THE
DEVIL'S TRAD

THE SPY FROM THE
WRECK

They both stared at the heap of golden guineas in baffled wonder. In the lamplight, the coins seemed to possess their own warmth – a fire that drew them in and robbed them of any desire to move or speak or leave that place. Will knew he wanted to keep this gold, to possess it, and he could see the same burning desire in Hannah's eyes. When she began to slip the guineas back into the leather purse, letting them trickle through her fist, he almost wanted to reach out and snatch it away from her.

"What are you doing?" he said.

"This way it will be easier to carry. Help me. We can hide the bag inside my basket."

"You mean *steal* it?"

Look out for Will's first breathtaking adventure...

The Sign of the Angel

THE DEVIL'S TRADE

THE SPY FROM THE
WRECK

ALAN MACDONALD

■SCHOLASTIC

To Lewis - the best reader and critic
anyone could ask for

Scholastic Children's Books,
Commonwealth House, 1–19 New Oxford Street,
London, WC1A 1NU, UK
a division of Scholastic Ltd
London ~ New York ~ Toronto ~ Sydney ~ Auckland
Mexico City ~ New Delhi ~ Hong Kong

First published by Scholastic Ltd, 2005

ISBN 0 439 96376 1

Printed and bound by Nørhaven Paperback A/S, Denmark

10 9 8 7 6 5 4 3 2 1

1

Shipwreck

All evening the storm had been gathering in the west, hanging over the village like a bad omen. At the Angel Inn, Will Finch had been crossing the back yard when he felt the wind drop and the air turn cooler. He had lived long enough by the sea to know its moods. This was only the breathing space – the lull before the storm would strike. He felt the leaden sky pressing in on him and hurried inside the inn, bolting the back door behind him, hugging his thin body against the cold.

The parlour was half empty that evening. Most of the men had read the storm in the heavy sky and stayed at home with their families. Will paused to watch Dr Rankin playing backgammon with his friend Dutch, who was leaning forward studying the pieces as if they were a puzzle. He was losing because he was thinking about his fishing boat, the *Flora*, down at the Stade, and hoping that it would be safe on the bank of shingle. Dr Rankin already had four of his black pieces home.

The rain came first, tapping on the window, then drumming steadily like an army on the march. At the sound men looked up from their drinks for a moment and exchanged glances, glad that they were safe in the dark, smoky parlour where Will's mother, Susannah Finch, served them hot rum. There would be no landing tonight, Will reflected gloomily. In the last month only one cargo had been brought home and the smugglers in Lydwell were running low on their stocks of spirits and tobacco.

For an hour the storm beat around the inn, the wind droning in the great brick chimney and sending clouds of smoke gusting into the parlour. Just after seven, long after the candles had been lit, the door banged open and a man came stumbling in, taking off his hat to shake off the rainwater that had collected in the brim. He had a lantern with him and when he lifted his head, Will recognized Jemmy Dunn, who kept a solitary farm a mile to the west of Lydwell, within sight of the coast.

"There's a ship in trouble!" Jemmy called out and the talk in the parlour died away. "The wind's driving it towards the rocks at Leonard's Cove. I seen the lights from my window. If you are men, come now, and pray heaven we're not too late!"

In no time the inn began to empty. Men threw on their coats and hats, took up their lanterns and bent their heads into the fierce, gusting wind as they stepped out into the street. They didn't want to go out into the storm but they had no choice: it was the law of the sea. Many of them were fishermen and knew that next week or next year it might be their own boat in distress. If the worst came to pass and the ship struck the reef, there might be a cargo to salvage – perhaps whale or seal oil, cork, timber, or even casks of spirits if they were lucky – but they didn't want to think about that now. First they would do whatever they could to save the lives of the poor wretches on board.

Dutch tipped back the last of his brandy and got to his feet. He was broad-shouldered and his head almost touched the beams of the low ceiling. Beside the portly, ruddy-faced doctor he looked like a giant.

Rankin buttoned his greatcoat and looked at Will. "Are you coming?" he asked.

Will looked at his mother, wanting her permission, but knowing that someone would have to stay behind to take care of the inn. Susannah Finch wiped her hands on her apron and sighed. "Go, if you must. Just don't do anything foolish."

* * *

3

By the time they reached the parade it seemed as if half the village had turned out and was heading towards Leonard's Cove. Will, Dutch and the doctor joined the crowd, hurrying along in the driving wind. Many of the villagers carried lanterns and some had brought ropes, which they wore slung over their shoulders. One man was driving a farm cart drawn by two dapple-grey horses and the crowd parted to let him through. Will saw children tugging anxiously at the hands of their parents, afraid that they might arrive too late – in a village like Lydwell a shipwreck was a great event that no one wanted to miss.

He recognized many of the men who gave a nod or a brief salute to Dutch and the doctor as they hurried by. Ahead of them he caught sight of the Reverend Spencer, striding along with one hand holding on to his black broad-brimmed hat. Holding on to his other arm and trying to keep pace with him was a girl he'd never seen before. She was wearing a long red cloak with the hood hiding her face. The hem of her dress was muddied and wet where she must have crossed the fields from the Rectory to reach the coast road. As Will drew almost level with her, she turned her face and caught him staring, so that he coloured and looked away. She was a girl about his own age, with dark hair framing a pale face and large brown eyes that stared back at him defiantly. Will wondered where she had appeared from. Visitors were rare in the village and he knew the Reverend Spencer lived by himself at the Rectory.

Leonard's Cove was a small inlet a mile to the east. It was rumoured that the beach was a haunt of smugglers, but Will knew that it was a hazardous place to attempt a landing because of the dangerous rocks protecting the cove. At low tide, a crescent of golden brown sand could be reached on foot via a steep path. But now the sand was hidden from sight and the tall cliff of Gammon Head guarded the bay at the far end. At the foot of the cliff a narrow causeway of rocks stretched out into the sea like a row of jagged black teeth, and it was towards this reef that the ship was being driven by the gale. On a calm spring day, Will had walked out to the end of the rocks, but never when the swell was running high and the waves were crashing over them in white breakers.

As they reached the cove he could see lights on top of the cliff, where a small knot of people had gathered. "There she is!" bellowed Dr Rankin, pointing out to sea. But Will had already seen it. The ship was past the headland and listing heavily to starboard, like a tree bending in the wind. In the south-westerly gale it was helpless as it was driven ever closer to the rocks and its inevitable doom. The waves around it were like grey mountains and, as they watched, the boat plunged down into a dizzying trough, only to appear again miraculously, borne up on the next wave. Will could see it was a brig of the old-fashioned style but it was barely recognizable from the vessel that must have put to sea. The sails – what was left of them – hung like cobwebs from the mast. All around, the sea was littered with pieces of copper sheathing that had broken loose from the bottom of the boat and floated away. Even from this distance Will could tell the brig was close to breaking up. It must have been fighting against the gale all evening, but with the sea running high and the wind right on the shore the anchor cable had broken, and now it was only a matter of time.

Climbing the back of Gammon Head, Will joined the onlookers gathered on top of the cliff. The crowd had swelled to sixty or more. They pressed close together, their heads bent against the stinging wind and rain and their eyes fastened on the black outline of the ship. It was close enough for them to see figures on board and sometimes hear shouts carried on the wind. The crew had seen the lights on the cliffs and were crying out for help.

"Can't we do anything, Uncle?"

Will looked around to see it was the girl in the red cloak who had spoken.

"Nothing, Hannah," replied the Reverend. "Only watch and pray."

"It would be madness to try and reach them in this

gale," Rankin said half to himself. "All they can do is hope to heaven she holds in one piece when she strikes."

"Then God have mercy," murmured Reverend Spencer and he began to mumble under his breath. It took Will a few moments to understand that the clergyman was praying. Several of the women standing close by bowed their heads too as a mark of respect. Will glanced at the girl but saw that she kept her eyes open and fixed on the ship, as if she believed its fate depended on her. The hood of her cloak had blown back, but she didn't seem to notice the rain that soaked her dark hair or ran down her face. She gazed out to sea, almost as if she could feel the terror of the people that were clinging to the doomed vessel.

Now they could see frantic activity on board. A rowing boat had been lowered into the water from the side as the ship rose and plunged with each new wave. Will found his eyes drawn to a man in a white shirt who seemed to be trying to rally the frightened crew. His hair was fair, almost golden, which made him easy to single out even from a distance. Will saw him hand a woman into the boat and pass a child into her outstretched arms. Others were trying to save their own skins, throwing themselves from the rails into the little boat. But the boat quickly became overcrowded and there was a danger it would sink under the weight of the people swarming into it. Even as the crew tried to row away from the side, men threw themselves into the raging sea in a desperate attempt to claw their way on board. But their efforts were all in vain – before the boat had travelled more than a cable's length, a wave rose up like a grey cliff and swept right over it, overturning the craft as if it was a piece of driftwood. On the cliff-top a groan escaped from the watching crowd and many of them turned their heads away, unable to watch. One of the younger children began to cry.

For more than an hour, Will watched the ship fight for its life, hoping for a miracle. But soon after nine o'clock it struck the reef with a terrible renting and splintering of timber. The jagged rocks tore through its broadside and the ship seemed to rear up on its keel like a frightened horse. He saw a man drop from the cross-trees and fall into the seething cauldron below.

The ship had impaled itself on a hidden reef, just beyond the end of the causeway. On the deck perhaps a dozen of the crew were left, but they couldn't reach the land without swimming across a forbidding expanse of icy black water. And now the sea began to beat against the stricken vessel seeking to swallow it once and for all. Waves swept over the deck in breakers as high as a house. Will could see the fair-haired man who seemed to be trying to lash himself to the main mast. Then he realized he was not lashing himself to it, but trying to cut it away with an axe. He kept at it with a will and was joined by two more of the crew. At last with a crack like thunder, the mast splintered and gave way. By luck or design, it fell towards the land, creating a floating bridge between the ship and the rocks, with the rigging drifting in the sea. The man was already urging the crew to abandon the ship and use the mast as a lifeline to reach the rocks. Some clung to the remaining fore-mast, stubbornly refusing to enter the water.

"Why don't they swim before it's too late?" asked Hannah.

"The rocks, Miss," replied Dutch, pointing. "They fear the rocks. Even if they reach them the waves will dash them to pieces."

Will guessed that, in any case, many of the crew couldn't swim and preferred to take their chances on the listing deck. They could see pieces of wreckage on the rocks that had been splintered in pieces by the lash of the breakers. Only the fair-haired man was undaunted. He stood at the rails and dived into the foaming water. For a moment Will thought he was lost, then he saw his head bob to the surface by the mast and he grasped it with both hands. He began to make his way along it, hand over hand, nimble as a monkey. Every breaker threatened to sweep him away but he clung to the mast tenaciously until the wave was past, and then inched forward once again. When they saw that he hadn't drowned, the remaining survivors on the deck took heart. One by one they climbed over the rails and threw themselves into the sea to try and reach the mast. But their delay was to prove fatal. The ship's ancient timbers could withstand no more. The rudder came away first, and then the ship seemed to crack open, so that the stern slid right away and the forecastle bucked and rose higher. With the sudden violent movement the fallen mast lurched and those clinging on to it were shaken loose like leaves in the wind. Will watched in horror as they struggled to regain their hold, then were swept away by the next incoming breaker and swallowed up. Only the golden-haired man clung on stubbornly, with his arms and legs wrapped round the mast. With the next gigantic breaker he finally lost his grip, but with a few swift strokes was able to reach the rocks. They could see him hanging on to the rocks at the end of the causeway, the shirt torn from his back so that he was naked apart from his breeches. There he lay, either spent or unconscious.

Hannah broke free of her uncle and went to the edge of the cliff. "We could reach him!" she pointed. "Quickly, before it's too late! Why are you all standing there?"

But the Reverend seized her arm and pulled her back from the edge. "Keep away, child. The rocks are treacherous. There's nothing to be done."

Her eyes burned with indignation. "You can't just leave him to die!"

"We'll not do that Miss, don't you worry." The tall figure of Dutch had appeared beside her, towering over the Reverend Spencer so that the parson took a step back in alarm. His face was set with grave determination. Among the smugglers of Lydwell, Dutch was the acknowledged leader, and where he led, others would follow. On an impulse, Will pushed his way through the crowd to the edge of the cliff.

"Don't be a fool, Will. Leave this to us," said Dr Rankin, who was already stripping off his coat. Will shook his head stubbornly and was rewarded by a smile of gratitude from Hannah. In that moment he felt he would do anything for this dark-haired girl.

Soon six of them were clambering down the cliff-face, armed with the ropes. The descent was difficult in the buffeting wind, but it was only when they reached the bottom that Will understood the peril of the task they were attempting. The rocky causeway stretched out some fifty yards beyond them to where the survivor hung on grimly. Every wave that came in threatened to prise his fingers loose and suck him back into the sea. Dutch had already knotted the two longest ropes together and tied one end around his waist. "Hold fast to me," he bellowed to them over the roar of the waves. "When you feel me tug on the rope, start to reel me in."

With that he set off towards the point, leaning into the driving wind. Will took up the rope with the other men. For a big man Dutch was surprisingly agile, and at first made good progress. But halfway out he reached a yawning gap between the rocks, where the sea rushed through in a swirling, black current. They saw him hesitate for a moment, then leap across the gap and cling to the face of a rock, just as another breaker licked over him. Then on he went, climbing over the next shelf of rock and disappearing at last from their sight.

There was nothing to do but wait and hope. Will kept his eye fixed on the point where Dutch had vanished. After what seemed an eternity he felt a strong tug on the rope they were holding. Dutch had reached his quarry and was coming back. When they came into sight Will had the impression of a two-headed giant coming towards them. As it drew closer he realized that Dutch was carrying a pale, half-naked creature on his back, the man clinging round his neck like a child. Dutch moved slowly, pausing each time one of the foaming breakers engulfed him and threatened to dislodge his footing. When he finally reached the gap between the rocks he stopped, faced with an impossible dilemma. With the man on his back he couldn't leap across – the gap was too wide and his burden too heavy – but his passenger was too weak to attempt the jump by himself. Will saw that they were trapped on a narrow ledge, with no way forward. Without thinking, he abandoned the rope he was holding and ran forward to try and help them. But even before he had gone a few steps he saw a towering wave leap and throw itself at the rock where they were clinging on for dear life. Dutch's foot slipped on the ledge, found thin air, and he tumbled forward into the sea with the man still clinging to his back.

"Pull!" bellowed Dr Rankin. "For the love of God, pull him in!"

Will's boots slipped and slid on the seaweed. Drenched to the skin and half-blinded by salt water, he fought his way forward to reach the channel. He could see the rope pulled taut, leading down into the water, and clinging to it was the survivor of the wreck, though with no sign of the one who had rescued him. If it hadn't been for the rope the swirling black current would have carried the man away, but Rankin and the others were slowly drawing him in like a fish on a line. Will grasped the rope to add his own strength. One more pull and the man was alongside, so Will could reach out and grasp him by the arm. Choking and retching, he came out and Will saw that his chest and shoulders were torn and bloodied where he had been battered against the rocks, trying to clamber ashore. Around his waist was tied the rope that had saved his life, the one that Dutch had worn around himself when he had set out. Will bent over the pale, exhausted figure.

"Where's Dutch?" he pleaded. "The man who carried you! Where is he?"

The man shook his head and closed his eyes.

"*Il est mort*," he groaned. "Drowned."

2

The Frenchman

Will awoke the next morning to find himself in his mother's bed. His mother was asleep, breathing deeply, with her back turned towards him. As he lay still, the events of the previous night came back to him like a bad dream. He saw again the ship being dashed on the rocks, the man clinging to the fallen mast, trying to reach the shore, and then Dutch slipping and falling, falling into the foaming sea. Dutch was dead and in the next room lay the man whose life he had saved – a Frenchman. They had brought him back to the village last night on the farm cart, semi-conscious and occasionally babbling words in his own strange language.

"A damned frog," Dr Rankin had shaken his head bitterly. ("If we'd known we should have left him to drown." In the end Will had taken pity on the foreigner and suggested they carry him into the Angel. The inn was close to the coast path and no one else seemed eager to take the stranger in, knowing it would mean an extra mouth to feed or perhaps a body that would eventually need burial. Susannah Finch had watched tight-lipped while they carried the man through the parlour and up the stairs to the front bedroom. Will had said nothing about him being French, afraid that she would turn him away. His mother would find out soon enough in the morning.

Now Will crept on to the landing, dressed in his nightshirt. The door to his bedroom was ajar and he looked in. At first he thought the Frenchman must have died in the night. His face was so pale that he could have been a corpse laid out for burial, but as Will went closer he could hear his shallow breathing. Will had never seen a Frenchman before. He had always imagined them to be brutish and ugly, but this man looked almost gentle as he slept. He had golden-brown hair that fell down to the nape of his neck below the bandage Dr Rankin had tied round his head. An inkblot of blood had seeped through the linen forming a crimson patch. So this was the enemy, Will thought, the enemy that everyone feared. He studied the Frenchman's face and wondered who he was. Last night he had spoken some words of English, which suggested he wasn't a common sailor. There was also the evidence of the scars Will had seen on his arms and his back. They were old and white, not fresh like the wounds he'd suffered from his ordeal on the rocks. This was a man who had survived battles of other kinds.

Later that morning he found his mother in the kitchen, stirring a pan of porridge.

"Our guest is awake," she said, and he heard the edge of anger in her voice. "Why didn't you tell me he was French?"

Will avoided looking at her. He cut himself a slice of the dark brown loaf.

"He needed help," he said evasively.

"Does anyone else know? Answer me, Will, do they know who he is?"

"No. I don't think so," replied Will. "He was barely alive when we brought him back."

"Well, I hope you are right, for both our sakes. I don't want the village knowing we're sheltering his kind. You keep it to yourself, Will. If anyone asks, he's a sailor, a plain honest English sailor."

"What does it matter? Someone had to take him in," said Will.

"Matter? Lord love you, boy! Have you been in a dream these past months? We are at war!"

"I know," said Will.

"Then use your head, we cannot keep him here!"

"It won't be for long. Just until he recovers. Please, he's nowhere else to go."

His mother ladled three slops of the porridge violently into a bowl. "I must be a fool," she muttered, shaking her head. "Throw him out on the street, that's what I should do, let the dogs lick his wounds."

Will knew his mother wasn't as callous as she pretended. Underneath her bluster she was soft-hearted and would help anyone in true need. All the same he noticed the breakfast that she gave him to take upstairs was no more than a bowl of the watery porridge with a slice of dry brown bread. His mother didn't intend to waste good eggs and butter on a Frenchman. As he carried the tray upstairs he thought about the war and the way it had changed their lives. For months now the country had been on a state of alert, alarmed by the rumours that Napoleon was gathering a great army across the channel. Like every other town and village along the south coast, Lydwell was in the grip of patriotic fever. Only the other evening, Will had seen a Recruiting Sergeant parading through the village with a drummer beating out a tattoo. Soldiers in the scarlet jackets of the infantry carried lighted torches and paper lanterns on tall poles that declared *God Save the King!*. Some of the younger men from the village had enlisted, including Danny Fallon who was fourteen, only a year older than Will himself. Secretly Will had day-dreamed of wearing a uniform himself and marching off to war with a musket over his shoulder, but he knew he couldn't leave his mother to manage the inn on her own. Besides, since last year when he'd discovered that half of the men in the village were members of a smuggling gang, his life had hardly been lacking in adventure.

He knocked softly on the door, and when there was no answer, went in.

The Frenchman's eyes blinked open, at once alert and suspicious, but when he saw the solemn-faced boy standing by his bed he relaxed.

"I brought you some breakfast," said Will. "Breakfast?" He held the bowl lower so the foreigner could see the food.

"Thank you," said the man, smiling. He tried to sit up in bed, but groaned and had to lay back. Will had to help him ease himself slowly upright and felt him wince with the pain of every movement. Once he was sitting up, he took the bowl from Will and began to eat hungrily, spooning the thin porridge into his mouth and wiping the flecks away from his mouth with the back of his hand. Will sat on a chair by the window and watched him with frank curiosity.

"How are you feeling now?" he asked, when the bowl was clean.

"Bruised." The Frenchman grinned back at him. "Here I am, eating my breakfast when we haven't been introduced. My name is Louis Moreau."

His English was surprisingly good, spoken precisely with a touch of formality and no trace of the Sussex burr that Will was used to.

"I'm Will."

"I don't think your mother cares much for me, Will."

Will shrugged. "You're French. She says if folk in the village find out, it could make trouble for us."

"She's right, Will, you should listen to her. By staying here I'm putting you in danger. And I have no right to ask for your help. I should leave as soon as possible."

"You can't even walk," said Will. "Dr Rankin says he thinks you've a cracked rib."

"I have felt better," admitted Louis. "But I haven't yet thanked you for saving my life. You're the boy who pulled me out of the sea?"

"It was Dutch who saved you," said Will. "The man who carried you on his back."

Louis's eyes widened at the memory. "Yes, I remember, the giant! I thought I was dreaming when I saw him coming over the rocks. This man, Dutch, he was a friend of yours?"

"Yes," said Will. "A friend." He looked down at the floor. It was impossible to explain who Dutch had been. A man they had all respected, relied on, who knew every inch of the coastline, every creek, bay and cove. Now he was gone, and he left a large space that would be hard to fill. Will couldn't say any of this, so he lowered his eyes and let the silence settle like dust in the room.

Louis was looking at him. "I'm sorry for your friend. Truly sorry," he said. "I tried to hold on to him in the water but the current. . ." He broke off and looked away. Will was surprised to see there were tears in his eyes for this stranger who had saved his life. *None of this is his fault*, thought Will. *He is lost in a strange country without friends or money.*

"Why were you on that ship?" Will asked.

"The *Fortune*? She was a merchant ship bound for Brighton."

"You were one of the crew?"

"No, I paid for my passage. It's complicated, Will, but if you like I will try to explain."

Will sat down on the end of the bed. He was supposed to be getting ready for school but today he would just have to be late.

"Perhaps I should start with my grandfather," Louis began. "He was an Englishman, like you. He had a large house in Brighton. You've been there many times, I suppose?"

Will shook his head. "I'd like to go one day. My

mother says they have shops with windows as big as our parlour."

Louis laughed. "Yes, shops, a thousand shops, like Paris. But my grandfather was a banker. Not as interesting as a shopkeeper, but it made him rich. I remember staying at his house when I was young, six or seven years old. To me it seemed like a king's palace. So many rooms, Will, you should have seen it! I used to wander for hours from room to room, just wanting to touch all these wonderful things – silver clocks and mirrors, musical boxes. . ."

Will could easily imagine this man as an eager, golden-haired boy. Even now he spoke with sudden bursts of enthusiasm, his face alight with memories.

"But my grandfather, I was telling you about him. He had only one child, a daughter. Her name was Emilia. At a ball in Brighton she met a Frenchman, Georges Moreau."

"Your father?" guessed Will.

"My father, a young officer, a nobody at that time. He took my mother to live in Paris, where a year later I was born. I hardly saw my English grandfather after that – the Revolution intervened and it was difficult for my parents to leave the country. But two months ago my mother had a letter – her father had died and left her the house in Brighton along with some money, a lot of money.

So you see, Will, that's why I had to come."

Will wasn't sure he did see. "Surely, with the war it's dangerous. Won't they put you in prison?"

"Perhaps. If they know I'm here," said Louis. He held Will's gaze for a moment. "But my mother is old now, Will, she lives by herself in a draughty apartment. All she talks about is her father's house in England. It's rightfully hers, but there are legal matters that have to be settled. Relatives of my grandfather are disputing the will."

Will frowned. "How can they? You said the house was left to her."

Louis's face clouded. "Wherever there's money people gather like flies, Will. They want to cheat my mother of her inheritance. That is why I had to come. When I heard of a merchant ship going to England, I persuaded the captain to take me along. My plan was to land in Brighton and go to the lawyers in secret. If I can prove my mother's claim to the house, I can settle the matter once and for all."

Will nodded. He wasn't sure he understood the difficulties over the will but he sympathized with Louis. The war had made things difficult for everyone. Louis had taken a great risk in coming, perhaps a foolish one, but Will could imagine how the matter of the will had dragged on for month after month. Perhaps his mother had begun to despair. Dr Rankin had told him of cases that had been drawn out for years on end, until all the money had been eaten away by lawyers' fees.

"What will you do now?" asked Will. "Brighton is more than thirty miles away. And you haven't any money."

Louis spread his hands in despair. "True. I lost everything when the *Fortune* went down. Everything. But I'm still alive. Perhaps I can still find a way to reach Brighton when I'm strong enough. You and your mother have been so kind to me, more than I deserve, and I bring you nothing but trouble."

"You can stay as long as you want," Will said impulsively. He was sure that with time his mother could be persuaded and he hoped to enlist Dr Rankin's support. Louis had nowhere else to go, and in any case, Will wanted to prolong his stay as long as possible. He liked the way the Frenchman took him into his confidence and spoke to him as an equal. He rose from the bed, knowing he had stayed too long talking.

"You're going?" said Louis.

"I have to be at school."

"Wait. There's one more thing you could do for me."

Will paused in the doorway, a little awkwardly. "If it's money. . ."

Louis waved this away. "Not money, something far

more important. When the ship went down I lost some letters. They belonged to my mother and without them it will be hard to prove her claim on the will. You understand?"

"You mean you'll have come all this way for nothing?" said Will.

Louis nodded. "That is why I need you to try and find them for me. Go back to the place where the ship went down. See if anything has been washed ashore."

Will looked doubtful. "They're probably at the bottom of the sea. And even if I found them, the letters would be ruined."

Louis shook his head. "Perhaps not, they were in a box, tied up in a piece of oilskin cloth. It's a chance in a thousand, I know, but you could search the rocks."

The Frenchman was leaning forward eagerly, his pale blue eyes pleading. Will made up his mind: school could wait until tomorrow. He would much rather go to Leonard's Cove and, following the shipwreck, he guessed he wouldn't be the only one to miss lessons that day.

"All right," he said. "I'll go now."

"Thank you, thank you," Louis sat back against his pillow again, as if an enormous weight had been lifted from his shoulders.

3

Prisoner of War

The shining sand of Leonard's Cove was littered with the debris of the wreck. Among the rockpools Will found shattered fragments of the ship's hull, spars and tangled webs of rigging. All along the beach articles of clothing had been washed up among the driftwood – hats, stockings, boots, and even a woman's white shift. (Will thought of the woman he had seen Louis handing into the rowing boat and wondered who she had been.) Further on among the rocks he found the body of one of the crew, slumped on his side with his face turned from the sky. His skin was so white and shiny that he looked like he was made out of wax. Flies buzzed around him, and as Will watched one settled on the dead man's ear. Will gave a shudder and passed on by quickly.

Since first light the villagers had come and gone, picking through anything of worth that could be salvaged from the wreck. Here and there lay broken barrels with the staves sticking up out of the sand like black claws. Will stopped to examine one and found it contained traces of salt.

By the coastal path he could see a flat-bedded cart, painted black and drawn by two horses. Inside were a pile of corpses, heaped one on top of the other like so many sacks of flour. Liney Roach, the village undertaker, had come to collect the bodies for burial. Will tried to avoid looking at what was inside the cart and waved to the white-haired old man without going over.

At the far end of the beach two small children were fishing in the shallows for anything of value. He walked towards them. As he drew nearer, the boy looked up and returned to a pile he'd left on the sand, guarding his treasures jealously. The girl – who looked like his younger sister – was dressed in a faded grey dress, bunched up above her knees so she could wade freely in the water. The lower part of her dress was already drenched. Will had seen them about the village and knew they were part of a tribe of brothers and sisters called Turner. Like others in the village, their parents didn't see the point of sending them to the charity school.

In the pile of scavenged wreckage Will saw a ship's

lantern, some pewter bowls and items of bedraggled clothes including an odd assortment of boots and shoes.

"That's ours!" warned the boy as Will looked it over. "We found it. You keep away!"

"Find anything good?" said Will, casually, scanning the pile for something that looked like a box.

"You keep away," repeated the boy, jutting out his chin. "We found 'em fair and square. Go and look for your own." But his sister had come out of the water and couldn't resist boasting over their prizes.

"This is liquor," she said, rapping on a half-anker barrel as big as her head. "Found it floating out beyond them rocks. Tom had to wade up to his waist to get it."

"My mother will tan me for getting my breeches wet," said Tom proudly. "But I don't care."

Will crouched down to look at the barrel. Mingled with the tang of salt water and wood was the sweet smell of brandy. He wondered if the *Fortune* had been carrying contraband in its hold. As a passenger, Louis might have been ignorant of the exact nature of the cargo.

"And we found something else," said the girl.

"No, Annie! I said not to tell," warned her brother. But it was too late, from under the pile of clothes the little girl drew out a slim wooden box with an ornate lid, inlaid with mother of pearl. Will tried to conceal his eagerness to look at it. If it was Louis's box of letters, the pair might be persuaded to give it up. What use was a bundle of foreign letters to them?

"What's in there?" he asked.

"Secret," said the girl. "You've to promise not to tell." Her brother was scowling at her.

Will solemnly gave his word. She opened the box and unwrapped something long and bright from a piece of cloth inside. "A beauty, ain't it?" she said, smiling up at Will through her fringe of dirty hair.

There were no letters, only a short-barrelled pistol that flashed in the hard morning light. The box was well-made and airtight, so that the gun seemed little damaged. Will couldn't take his eyes off it. Most pistols he had seen were simple flintlocks but this one gleamed with polished brass and steel. The muzzle was short and the butt elegantly curved, ending in a round brass cap as bright as a diamond.

"What are you going to do with it?" he asked.

The boy, Tom, scratched his bare arm. "Sell it," he said. "Must be worth a lot, I reckon."

Will looked at the pistol critically. "Probably no use now," he said. "It wouldn't fire. Been in the water too long." In fact the pistol was so beautifully crafted that he had wanted it from the moment it was unwrapped. It was small enough to fit snug in a coat pocket and no one would know it was there. Some of the smugglers he knew – like Liney Roach – carried pocket knives, but a pistol might prove a handy thing.

Tom was putting it back in the box. "We'll take it to a shop," he said. "Might get a guinea for it."

He gave Will a calculating look.

"I'll give you a shilling," said Will.

The boy gave a derisive snort and wiped his mouth with the back of his hand. "Worth ten at least, I reckon. That's what we'd get in a shop."

"Which shop?" said Will. There were no gunsmiths in the village. The boy pretended not to hear. Will felt in his pocket. Three shillings was all the money he had. Two weeks ago he had been paid a guinea for his part in a cargo of tea the smugglers had landed at Ladder Bay, but he'd given fifteen shillings to his mother and now three was all that remained.

"Two shillings," he offered.

The boy shook his head stubbornly.

Will reluctantly drew out the three shillings from his pocket and weighed them in the palm of his hand. "Three shillings, then. That's all I have."

The boy stared down at the coins, biting his lip. His younger sister was tugging at his arm. Three shillings would buy a loaf of bread with money to spare for cheese or milk.

"Keep it then," said Will. "I don't want it anyway."

He turned and walked away, hoping that he hadn't miscalculated. After he'd gone a short distance, the little girl's feet came pattering across the sand, running after him.

"Wait! Tom says you can have it for three shillings!" She smiled at him and held out her upturned palm for the money. Will handed it over and walked away with his prize, feeling its weight in the box. Already he was planning where he could hide it.

On his return, he slipped upstairs to his bedroom to see Louis. The Frenchman was awake and eager to see him.

"You found them?" he asked.

Will shook his head. "I'm sorry. I searched all along the shore, but there was no sign of them. They must have gone down with the ship."

A shadow of anxiety crossed the Frenchman's face. He had obviously pinned his hopes on Will finding his mother's letters, even though he knew it was unlikely. On an impulse, Will decided to show him the prize he had brought back. He brought the slim box out from under his jacket and laid it on the bed, removing the ornate lid. In the morning light spilling through the window, the pistol looked more beautiful than ever.

Louis took it out and held it in the palm of his hand, judging its weight and balance. "Where did you get this?"

"Some children fished it out of the water. I bargained for it and paid them three shillings."

31

"It's a fine pistol." Louis pointed the barrel towards him. "You know how to fire it?"

Will tried not to look alarmed. He knew the pistol wasn't loaded but it was unnerving just the same. Louis smiled and lowered the gun. "That is your first lesson. A gun is not a toy, never point it at anyone unless you're prepared to fire. I will be your teacher if you like. How old are you, Will?"

"Thirteen."

"Old enough. I was ten when I first fired a pistol. But if you're to learn, we'll need powder and shot. Can you get them?"

Will said he could. He'd seen ammunition in the smugglers' storeroom, hidden beneath St Michael's graveyard. It could be reached via a secret passage that led from the cellar of the Angel. One night he would slip down there and take what he needed; no one would be any the wiser.

"What about your mother?" asked Louis. "Does she know about this? I see from your face she doesn't. Never mind, we'll find somewhere to hide it. It will be our secret, Will. Yours and mine."

They hid the pistol among the straw of the mattress, concealed in its ornate box.

Will could imagine his mother's reaction if she ever found it. She already worried whenever a smuggling run was planned, and Will knew that she lay awake to listen for his return in the early hours of the morning.

She would never approve of him carrying a pistol. Yet the weapon had already acquired a hold on his imagination. He didn't how it had come to survive the shipwreck, but it had come to him, this small mysterious treasure, and he was determined to keep it.

4

Incomer

Miss Parkes's Endowed School was run in the upstairs room of a former block-and mast-maker's shop at the top of the village. It was a gloomy building. Spidery cracks ran across the walls of the classroom and the sun rarely penetrated through the tall dusty windows at the back. Outside was a yard where the children were allowed out to play once a day. In the schoolhouse they sat in four rows on long forms – benches long enough to seat seven or eight children. Two rows faced each other on either side of the class, with Miss Parkes's tall desk – rather like a pulpit – raised on a platform at the front of the room. Miss Parkes liked order in her class. She was a small woman who wore a white day cap tied firmly under her chin. Sitting on her high stool she looked rather like a glass-eyed doll, but her charges had learned to their cost that she was always watching them. Anyone who broke her rules was swiftly punished.

The next day, lessons were interrupted early on by footsteps climbing the stairs and a knock at the door. Will was surprised to see the Reverend Spencer, who rarely came to the school or showed any interest in the children's education. He was accompanied by his niece. Hannah was wearing a clean white muslin dress, tied with a blue sash at the waist, and a matching ribbon in her dark hair. She stood at the front of the class while Miss Parkes hopped down from her high stool, fluttering round the clergyman like an eager sparrow. Hannah looked at the bare wooden floor, swept clean by one of the older girls that morning, and endured the rows of faces staring at her. She wished that her uncle would stop talking so that she could take her place with the others. Will had last seen her on the night of the shipwreck. From the back of the class he tried to catch her eye, but if she was aware of him she gave no sign.

When the Rector had gone, Miss Parkes turned to the class. "This is Hannah Burrell, Reverend Spencer's niece," she informed them. "While she is staying at the Rectory, she will be coming here to join us. I trust we will *all* do our best to make her feel welcome."

There was a murmur of assent from the class, but as Hannah made her way to her place, Will noticed some of the girls imitating the prim set of her mouth. Already the spotless muslin had caught their attention, outshining their cheap cotton-print dresses. They disliked her instinctively, for no better reason than that she was an "incomer" from another village.

Later that morning, when Hannah was given the privilege of handing out the slates, knowing looks were exchanged. It was plain that Hannah was going to be the teacher's new favourite, the one who would be singled out for rare words of praise. The Reverend Spencer wielded a great deal of influence in the village and Miss Parkes thought it wise to treat his niece kindly.

Sitting directly behind Hannah was Robert Newson, a fleshy, dull-witted boy, who was the same age as Will. As the morning went on Newson eyed the blue ribbon tied in Hannah's hair and longed to pull it loose. When the teacher's head was bent over her book, Hannah felt the tug on her hair and darted a furious look over her shoulder. The second time Newson pulled harder, and instead of crying out, Hannah spun round in a fury and punched him hard on the arm. He let out a surprised yell.

Miss Parkes looked up from the book on her desk. "Robert Newson, was that you?"

"No, Miss Parkes. She punched me!"

"Is this true, Hannah? I will not tolerate such behaviour in my class. Stand at your desk. You too, Robert Newson. On your feet, you insolent boy!"

"I'm sorry, Miss Parkes," said Hannah. "I lost my temper."

"Then you will learn to control yourself in future. I'm sure your uncle would be shocked to learn how you behave on your first day in school. Now, why did you hit that boy?"

Hannah hesitated.

"Come girl, speak up! I asked you a question!"

"He pulled my hair," replied Hannah softly.

"Speak up!"

"He – pulled – my – hair."

"Did he indeed? You may sit down, Hannah. Robert Newson, come out to the front."

Newson's mouth gaped open. Surely the new girl wasn't going to go unpunished? He made his way to the front of the class, the smirk gone from his face. A silence had settled over the class. The younger children in the front row – some only five or six years old – watched in appalled fascination as Miss Parkes took down the long slender cane which hung on the wall as a perpetual warning. Some of the older ones stared accusingly at Hannah. She was responsible for this. It was an unwritten rule that none of them ever split on another class member. They had learned that a dumb silence was their most effective weapon against Miss Parkes's tyrannical regime. But Hannah was new to the school and too outspoken, too quick to react. Will could tell from her face that she regretted having told the truth.

"Please, Miss Parkes. . ." she began, half rising from her place.

"Quiet!" barked the teacher furiously. "I will *not* have interruptions!"

Robert Newson knew from experience there was no point in protests, which would only increase the punishment. He held out his hand. His eyes were screwed up tight in his pink fleshy face, so that Will thought he looked more than ever like a pig. The hand he held out was trembling slightly.

Miss Parkes brought the thin cane down so quickly that it made the air hum. The whole class flinched at the smack of the birch on flesh. Newson drew his burning hand away but clenched his mouth so as not to cry out.

"Again," said Miss Parkes.

Once again, he offered his palm and again the cane came down. Again there was no cry, though the blood had drained from his face and his eyes were smarting with pain. Just before the third blow, he turned his head away from the teacher and his eyes met Hannah's. She saw the fury and resentment in that look, the promise that, however long it took, he would pay her back.

* * *

After school, Will saw Hannah walking quickly down Market Street by herself. On an impulse he ran to catch up and fell into step beside her. "I saw you on the cliffs, the night of the shipwreck," he said.

Hannah glanced at him. "I remember you," she said. "The boy who climbed down to the rocks."

"Yes," said Will. He waited for her to add something about how brave he had been helping to rescue Louis, but she didn't. They walked on in silence for a while.

"What became of him? I've been wondering," she asked.

"He's getting better," said Will. "He has a cracked rib, that's what Dr Rankin says. He's sleeping in my room at the Angel for now."

"The Angel?" She looked at him blankly.

"The Angel Inn. You must have seen it in the village. It's on Angel Lane just under the West Hill. My mother's the landlady."

Hannah shook her head. She'd hardly explored the village since her arrival. Her uncle didn't approve of her being out on her own. She glanced back at the groups of children coming down the lane from the school. "What's his name?"

Will almost said Louis but checked himself just in time. "Richard," he said. "His name's Richard Smith. He was the bosun's mate."

Behind them he caught sight of Robert Newson,

walking home with one of his cronies, a younger boy called Jack Merrit. They seemed to be keeping Hannah in sight. Will heard Newson's braying laugh in response to some whispered comment from Merrit.

"Wouldn't you rather be with your friends?" asked Hannah, following his gaze.

Will shook his head. "They're not my friends. But you should watch out for Newson. He won't forget what happened today. I saw the way he looked at you."

Hannah tossed her head dismissively. "Why should I care about him?"

Will felt exasperated. It was impossible to help this girl. "It's just a warning. You should watch out for him."

"Thanks," said Hannah. "But I can take care of myself." She stopped and pointed down the winding alleyway that cut along the side of the Customs House. "This is the way I go."

"Oh. Then I'll see you at school tomorrow."

"I suppose you will," she replied. "And by the by, that man who is staying at your house, his name isn't Richard."

"How do you know?"

"Because Richard is not a French name."

Hannah had slipped down the alleyway, but she looked back over her shoulder and smiled for the first time, pleased at the look of astonishment on his face.

Will walked on down Market Street towards home, feeling annoyed with himself. Why had he bothered to talk to Hannah in the first place? She was new to the village and he'd felt sorry for her, that was all. But it was quite obvious she hadn't given him a thought since the night of the shipwreck. To her he was just another boy from the village school, a boy who lived at a tavern with his mother and led a dreary life serving at tables. She couldn't know that he had another life, where he knew the name of every smuggler in the village and was trusted with their secrets. Will wondered how she would react, this proud disdainful girl, if he told her the Angel Inn was a haunt of smugglers and he was one of them. Of course, he could never tell her anything of the kind, he had sworn an oath of secrecy and Dr Rankin had warned him many times about the danger of careless talk.

From now on, Will decided, the Rector's niece could fend for herself. If she didn't have a single friend in the village, that was no fault of his. He'd tried to befriend her, to warn her about Robert Newson, but she hadn't listened. Well then, let her see how she fared on her own. It was nothing to him. He recalled her pleased smile as she glanced back over her shoulder. How could she have known that Louis was French? For if Hannah knew, then she might not be the only one in the village. It was a disturbing thought. Perhaps someone else had heard Louis babbling in his own language, the night they had carried him back to the village in the back of the farm cart. His mother had warned him there would be trouble if the word got round. As he reached the bottom of Market Street Will increased his pace. He was thinking of the powder and shot he needed for the pistol hidden in the straw of the mattress.

5

Arrest

Arriving home, Will found his mother in a state of nervous anxiety. He could hear voices coming from the back room and she ushered him into the hall, out of earshot.

"Make haste and run up to the doctor's house," she said. "Tell him he's needed urgently."

"Why? What's wrong?" asked Will.

"Lieutenant Lock – he's in there now with his men," she nodded towards the snug. "They're supping their drinks, but they're armed and it's your friend upstairs they've come for."

"But he's still weak, he can't even walk!" said Will.

"Much they care about that," said Susannah bitterly. "If you want to help him, fetch the doctor and hurry. I'll do my best to keep them downstairs."

*   *   *

Ten minutes later Will was hurrying back down
Market Street in the company of Rankin, who strode
along beside him with his old brown leather bag in
one hand.

"Let us hope we're not too late," said Rankin. "I
wondered how long before Lock would come sniffing
round."

"What will happen to Louis if he's arrested?" asked
Will.

"Prison," said the doctor flatly. "I was in Rye last
week and I saw a hulk moored on the river, a rotting
carcass of a ship they're using for prisoners of war. The
poor wretches on board are half starved, catching rats
to cook on their fires. They're kept in chains and live
most of their lives below decks, like moles in the dark."

Will imagined Louis left to this fate. "But Louis isn't
a prisoner of war," he argued.

"He's French, that's reason enough. Right now the
French are the very devil, Will, with horns and cloven
feet to prove it. You may shake your head but that's
the kind of thing I hear in the village every day."

"They don't know him," said Will. "I've talked to
him and he means us no harm."

"That's not the question," replied the doctor. "I
may be fond of a dog but it can still bite my hand. All
I am saying is you know nothing about him, nothing
at all. Only that he claims to have some business in

44

Brighton and seems in a desperate hurry to get there."

"Then you'd let them carry him off to prison? To starve to death?"

"I didn't say that," said the doctor. "I'll do what I can for him. But remember, I'm only a plain country doctor, Will, not a magistrate. Lieutenant Lock does what he pleases and there's little I can do about it. Besides, the fellow hates the sight of me."

Will knew this was true. The Lieutenant strongly suspected that the doctor was involved in the free-trade, but so far he had yet to find any proof. Nevertheless, Will clung to the hope that if anyone could save Louis, the doctor was the man. Turning into Angel Lane they came in sight of the inn and hurried towards it, hoping that they were in time.

As they climbed the stairs Will could hear his mother's voice raised in protest and the cold penetrating tones of Lieutenant Lock answering her. Lock was the most hated man in Lydwell. No one liked an Excise man and, as the District Riding Officer, Lock poked his nose into everyone's business. On his arrival in Lydwell he had boasted that he would put an end to all smuggling for thirty miles around, but so far he had only one haul of contraband to show for his effort. Lately – to the smugglers' satisfaction – the war had taken up much of the Lieutenant's time, since his appointment as second-in-command of the local volunteer force, grandly calling themselves the Lydwell Sharpshooters. Every weekday morning at six o'clock, Lock marched the volunteers through the streets of the village accompanied by the beating of drums and the playing of fifes, so that Dr Rankin had grumbled that if the French ever invaded, they would probably be driven away by the infernal racket. In the evening, anyone passing Priory Meadows could hear the pockpock of single muskets followed by ragged volleys of shots on the Lieutenant's barked command. The Lydwell Sharpshooters so far boasted only forty men, and some of them were almost as old as Squire Stanton, their commander, but they were all filled with a fervent desire to defend their country against the invader.

They found Lieutenant Lock in the bedroom with two of the volunteers, wearing their new dark green jackets. Not all of the volunteers possessed uniforms but those who did wore them with pride.

"Thank God you've come, Doctor," said Susannah as they entered. "The Lieutenant here was about to drag this poor man from his bed."

"Good day to you, Doctor," said Lock frostily. "I trust you haven't come to obstruct me in my duty. This fellow is a prisoner of war and, as I have explained, he must be handed over to the proper authorities for interrogation."

As ever, Lock spoke as if he was delivering a public lecture. With seven of them crowded into the small bedroom, the room felt stuffy and airless. Will and Rankin had to stand by the door, with only a few feet between them and the bed. Louis himself lay silently in the bed looking up at them. His head was still bandaged and there was a fine stubble on his chin, but considering he was about to be arrested, Will thought he looked remarkably calm.

"On whose orders?" asked Rankin.

"Major Stanton's," replied Lock.

"Poppycock!" returned the doctor. "Squire Stanton has no authority. Just because he calls himself major-general of your ragamuffin army doesn't give him the right to arrest any fellow he chooses."

Lock bristled. "Have a care what you say, Doctor. We are here on the King's business."

"I'll say what I damn well please," returned Rankin curtly. "And this gentleman is my patient. He cannot be moved unless I judge he is fit."

Lock sighed deeply. "You are trying my patience," he said. "My orders are to arrest this man. Carry him downstairs."

The two volunteers stepped forward and seized the startled Louis under his arms. As they dragged him up from under the blankets, he let out a howl of anguish that was loud enough to wake the dead. They were so startled that they let go of him immediately.

47

"I beg you, sirs!" panted Louis. "I beg you, do not try to move me again."

Lock looked at Rankin in astonishment. "Why the scoundrel speaks perfectly good English! What the devil is wrong with him?"

"Two of his ribs are broken, Lieutenant. He cannot walk nor scarcely move an inch without pain. What is more, there's a danger the stomach wall may be ruptured."

"Confound your medical nonsense!" said Lock. "In plain English, is he going to die?"

"In my opinion it would be a great mistake to move him. Rattling around in some confounded coach might be the end of him."

Will had been listening with alarm, but now he guessed that the doctor was exaggerating Louis's condition in an attempt to save him.

Lock approached the bed warily. "Where did you learn English, sir?"

"In England, sir," said Louis with a faint smile. "I spent much of my childhood not far from here in Brighton. But I will gladly answer all your questions another day, for now I beg you to let me rest. As you can see, in my present condition I am unlikely to attempt an escape."

Lock grunted. He hadn't bargained for the Frenchman being a gentleman. It changed things altogether – he couldn't be treated like a common prisoner; his life might be worth something, especially if he turned out to be a high-ranking officer. It would be intriguing to interrogate this man himself, to find out what he was doing here. He was good at worming the truth out of people and it couldn't do any harm to keep him at the Angel a little longer, before handing him over to the army. As for Squire Stanton, he was an old fool and could easily be won round to Lock's way of thinking.

Lock turned to the doctor. "How long before he's fit to walk?"

"That depends on his progress, Lieutenant. A week, perhaps two. He needs complete rest."

"Very well then, I grant you a week's stay. You will attend him daily, Doctor, and make it your business to see he makes a swift recovery. In the meantime one of my men will be stationed at the inn to guard the prisoner day and night."

"You're not billeting one of your rabble on me!" protested Susannah. "I've got one extra mouth to feed already. And besides, we have only the two rooms, there are no more beds to be had."

"I said nothing of beds, he can remain in the parlour downstairs. Those are my orders, Madam," said Lock stiffly. He turned to Louis. "I will come back to see you again, sir, and then we shall have more leisure to talk. Yes, I shall look forward to it."

6

Torches

Over the next week, Louis began to recover his strength. Dr Rankin said that his ribs were mending well but he should continue to wear the corset of bandages and try to rest. In the meantime, he should build up his strength and make the most of Susannah Finch's cooking. In prison he would not eat so well, nor half so often.

In the long November afternoons, when the light was fading rapidly, Will could often be found in his old room, sitting on the edge of the bed and talking to the prisoner. Having spent all his life in Lydwell, he had never met anyone as intelligent or interesting as Louis Moreau. Dr Rankin was the only other educated man he knew, but Rankin didn't live in Paris and hadn't been a soldier or lived through the horrors of the Revolution.

Louis told Will of the green-shuttered house where he lived on the Rue de Madeleine and the small garden where his daughter, Celeste, had first learned to walk. He described the bustling coffee-houses and elegant restaurants of Paris, the theatres and bookshops, now overflowing with the collections of rich families who had fallen into poverty. There was even a shop in the *Palais Royal* where an assistant would black your shoes while you rested them on a box and read the newspaper. To Will – who had never ventured far from his own village – it was as if he was walking through the streets of Paris, that strange gaudy city, with Louis beside him as his guide.

One day Will told Louis about the Rector's niece and how she kept herself aloof and had no friends at the schoolhouse. Louis listened with interest.

"Have you tried to talk to her?" he asked.

"Once, but she didn't want my help. She doesn't speak to anyone."

"Perhaps she is unhappy," suggested Louis. "You said she is staying with the priest?"

"Reverend Spencer," said Will.

"But where are her parents? Are they still alive?"

"I don't know. My mother says she's from Kent, a village in the marshes."

"There lies your answer. She's living in a strange place, among people she doesn't know. Perhaps she wishes she was home." He looked out of the window, at the grey English sky and the rain that had started to fall, and Will knew he was thinking not of Hannah but himself.

Every morning and evening, James Debney, the young volunteer Lock had left at the Angel, came upstairs to check on the prisoner. Debney was a stolid youth of nineteen who was proud that he had been chosen to guard the Frenchman. They always had ample warning of his approach, because he came clumping up the stairs in his hobnailed boots, whistling tunelessly to himself. Louis took great delight in exaggerating his fragile health whenever poor Debney appeared.

"Well, and how is the Frencher today?" Debney would ask the same question every day, standing in the doorway, with his head cocked on one side.

"You can see for yourself," Will would reply.

Louis, who had been talking animatedly only the minute before, now lay on his pillow with his eyes half closed and an expression of listless pallor, as if he was close to death's door. But as soon as Debney's footsteps had retreated downstairs, he would sit up, cock his head on one side and give a perfect imitation of Debney's low, husky voice.

Four days after his first visit, Lieutenant Lock came back and spent an hour upstairs, questioning the Frenchman. When the Riding Officer had gone,

Will found Louis out of bed for the first time. He was staring out of the window, with a troubled expression.

"I must leave here, Will, you know that, don't you?" he said.

"When?" said Will.

"Soon. If I stay, that man Lock will come back to hand me over to your English army. He believes I am a spy."

"A spy?" Will looked at the frail figure by the window with the purple scar on his temple, where the bandage had recently been removed. He was still wearing his borrowed nightshirt, and his bare feet were peeping out below it. It was typical of Lock, thought Will, to jump to such an absurd conclusion on so little evidence. Louis was French and could speak English, therefore he must be a spy.

"Didn't you tell him about your grandfather's house?" asked Louis.

"Of course, but he doesn't believe me. He says he will make his own enquiries. No, I must escape while I still have the chance. Before they throw me into some filthy cell or pass a worse sentence."

Will guessed he meant the gallows. Men had been hanged for as little as thieving; a Frenchman convicted of spying could hope for little mercy from a military court. Louis turned from the window.

"Can you help me, Will?"

Will hesitated. He had known that sooner or later Louis would think of escape. There was a secret he could tell him, but could he trust him with it?

Mistaking his silence, Louis smiled sadly. "I understand, you've done enough for me already. It's too much to ask."

"It's not that. It will be safer to go at night," said Will.

"I agree. Tonight, then."

"Tonight? You're not well enough. You can hardly walk."

Louis demonstrated this wasn't true by walking back and forth across the room, though he moved stiffly, like an old man riddled with gout. Will could tell that every step cost him pain, but knew that it would be futile to try to persuade him to wait. Any day now Lock might decide that he was fit to be moved and hand him over to the army.

For the next hour they made plans for Louis's escape. Will knew of a cave along the coast, beyond the abandoned lime kilns, where Louis could hide until they thought of somewhere more permanent. He went through the directions several times so that Louis was sure he could find the place once he was on the coast path. Debney remained a problem, but they decided to wait until after midnight in the hope that the young guard would be asleep.

* * *

Throughout the evening, Will helped his mother in the parlour. He kept an eye on Debney who stayed in his usual place in the corner nearest the hall where he could watch both the stairs and the front entrance. On the first day the young recruit had stood stiffly on guard, but by now he allowed himself to sit at a table, and accepted an occasional sip of rum to warm himself.

At eight o'clock, Will went upstairs to take Louis a bowl of broth for his supper. Under his jacket, he hid half a loaf of bread, some cheese and a bottle of brandy, bundled inside a cloth. Louis thanked him for the provisions and was even more delighted with the powder and shot that Will had purloined from the smugglers' storeroom the previous night. "You are a magician, Will!" he laughed. "Where did you find this?"

"It doesn't matter," said Will. He felt inside the mattress and pulled out the pistol in its case, handing it to the Frenchman. "Take this," he said. "If anything goes wrong you may need it."

Louis thanked him and began to load the pistol, quickly and efficiently. As Will watched him, he heard a distant booming noise, coming from somewhere down in the village. At first he thought it was gunfire from the battery, and wondered if tonight of all nights, the invasion had begun. Then he caught the rhythm, a steady repeated note, the thud of a drum coming nearer. The sound made Louis stiffen and look up, but he carried on loading the pistol until he was satisfied it was ready.

Will went to the window and pulled the curtain aside, peering along the empty street. The first thing he saw was the yellow glare of the torches. A crowd was coming up the hill. Most of them were young men, a few wearing the green jackets of the volunteers. They were armed with clubs or sticks. A handful of women swelled the numbers of the crowd to fifty or more so that they filled the narrow lane. At the head of the mob, the youth with the drum beat loudly in military time so that the sound echoed off the roofs and set dogs barking in the street. The crowd seemed to be incensed by the drum's rhythm and the murmur of their voices rose higher.

"Who are these people?" asked Louis.

"I don't know," said Will. "Perhaps it's a parade."

But in his heart he knew that this was no orderly march. There was no sign of Lieutenant Lock, or Squire Stanton riding his white horse. This was a rabble, a drunken mob, intent on some mischief. He hoped that they would pass on by but they seemed to be making straight for the Angel.

"I have seen people like this in Paris," said Louis. "Like a pack of dogs. Once they're in this mood you cannot reason with them." He blew out the lamp, plunging the room into darkness.

Below them the crowd had come to a halt outside the inn, under the sign which creaked back and forth in the wind. Will wondered if he ought to go downstairs to warn his mother. Surely she would have heard the commotion and bolted the front door to keep them out? His mother had been right, Will reflected. She had warned there would be trouble if word got round the village and now trouble had come to their door.

One of the mob, a woman with long grey hair, was holding a burning torch to something. She raised it aloft on a pole so it was just below the window where they were standing.

Will could see it was a tattered flag, a French tricolour. It burned quickly in a bright plume to wild cheering from the crowd and when it was done, they danced on the ashes that fell to the ground. Then the deafening thud of the drum began again, a death-knell increasing in rhythm while the crowd beat their sticks and clubs on the ground so that it sounded like an earthquake. The noise reached a crescendo and at its height one of the volunteers fired a musket in the air.

"Bring him down!" cried a voice. "Bring out the French son of a whore!" Others took up the cry using coarser language. Someone threw a stone and it splintered one of the parlour windows.

They heard quick footsteps on the stairs and

Susannah Finch threw open the door of the bedroom, looking pale and shaken.

"You hear that, sir? It's you they've come for! You see what comes. . ."

She took a step back and put a hand over her mouth. "Lord save us! Where did you get that? Will, come away from there!"

Louis looked a strange figure as he stood by the window in his long white nightshirt, with the pistol in his hand.

"Please don't be alarmed, Madame," he said, "I promise you I mean you no harm. If we all keep our heads, perhaps there is some way out of this."

"What way?" said Susannah. "If you go out there, they'll tear you to pieces. And if you stay here, sooner or later they'll break in and kill us all. Can't you hear them beating on the door?"

"Is there a back way?" asked Louis.

"Too late," said Susannah. "They're out in the yard too."

Louis muttered something in his own language that might have been a curse. "Then there's no other choice. I must go down and face them."

"No!" said Will. "There's another way."

His mother shot him a warning glance. She guessed what he had in mind.

"It's his only chance," said Will. "We have to tell him."

"Please," said Louis. "Whatever it is, we haven't much time."

Will made up his mind. Perhaps it was dangerous to trust Louis with the inn's secret, but he had to take the risk. He had heard of lynchings taking place and he had no wish to see what the crowd outside would do to Louis if they laid hands on him.

"Listen," he said, "there is another way out of here. Behind the barrels in the second chamber of the cellar, you'll find a hidden door. It's the entrance to a tunnel which leads under the West Hill. Follow the passage and you'll come out in the graveyard at St Michael's. From there you can reach the cliffs and the place I told you about."

"We are trusting you with this," said Susannah. "If you ever breathe a word. . ."

"You have my word," said Louis. "But we need to move quickly."

"What about Debney?" asked Susannah.

With the arrival of the mob, Will had quite forgotten about the young volunteer downstairs.

"Bring him up here," said Louis. "Perhaps he may be able to help us."

James Debney was crouched behind the bar with his musket trained on the front door, trying to keep his hands from shaking. He could hear the mob outside – their din was like a continuous roar in his ears punctuated by the beating of their fists and muskets against the door. Even with the barricade of tables and benches he had built against it, he knew it was only a matter of time before they broke in. He hadn't decided yet whether he would open fire. Lieutenant Lock had told him to prevent the prisoner escaping, but he hadn't said what to do if an angry mob broke in and dragged the Frenchman outside. In any case what in God's name *could* he do – one man against a hundred? (He had already begun to rehearse what he would say in his own defence.) Some of the men outside were his friends in the volunteers – he had seen Arton Hughes through the window, beating his drum. No, he wouldn't shoot, he would appeal to them calmly to go home – and if they wouldn't listen, well, let them take the damned Frog and have done with it. Why should he risk his own neck? The door at the end of the hall jumped on its hinges, interrupting his thoughts and bringing him back to the present.

"Mr Debney! Come quickly, sir! It's the prisoner!"

The voice from upstairs sounded urgent, alarmed. It was the landlady's boy calling down to him. Debney abandoned his post gladly and went thumping up the stairs in his hobnailed boots, the musket clasped in his hands. When he came through the door he saw an empty bed with the blankets strewn in a heap. The boy and his mother were standing by the window, staring at him as if transfixed. For a moment, he thought the Frenchman must have leapt out of the window to his death. Then he heard the click of the pistol, and felt the cold muzzle press hard into the back of his neck.

"Now, my young friend," said the voice in his ear. "I have no wish to kill you, so put the musket down on the bed. Good. And the pistol from your belt. Now strip off your clothes and do it quickly."

Will clattered downstairs to the parlour with his mother behind him, hoping that they were not too late. He could hear the mob crashing the butts of their muskets against the front door, trying to break in. A moment later a crack came from the hall as the hinges finally gave way. But the barricade of tables held them up a little longer.

He stood at the foot of the stairs with his mother beside him. She had taken the heavy iron poker from the fireplace and was gripping it tightly. Will hoped that upstairs Louis was hurrying.

They came pouring into the parlour, the drummer at their head, in his green jacket – a youth of no more than twenty with a wild-eyed look about him. Arton Hughes advanced on them with one of the burning torches in his hand. The scent of burning tallow filled the room and the smoke blackened the ceiling. Will knew that if he was provoked, he could set the whole place ablaze.

"Where is the furriner? Where have you hidden him?" he demanded.

"You've come to the wrong house. There's no foreigners here," said Susannah. "I think you should all go home before Lieutenant Lock arrives."

The youth came up close to her so that she could feel the heat from the torch and smell the beer on his warm breath. "Lady, I don't give a tinker's cuss what you think. We've come for that foreign scum. We know he's here, so don't try and lie to me."

The grey-haired old woman pushed her head between them. "Maybe she's got a taste for the Frogs? Upstairs is he, dear? In your bed?"

"I told you he isn't here," said Susannah, ignoring the crude laughter.

"Then we'll find him ourselves," said the youth. "And when we do, we'll string him up. I hear the Frenchers like to dance, well, let's see how he dances with a noose round his neck!"

Hughes lowered the torch in his hand so the flames cast a flickering light across Susannah's face. Will saw the fear in his mother's eyes and caught hold of the hand holding the torch.

"Leave my mother alone," he said distinctly.

Things might have turned ugly then, if the figure in the green jacket hadn't appeared at the top of the stairs. "Up here!" he shouted. "Quickly!"

Hughes wrenched his arm free and joined the mob,

who were already pushing their way towards the stairs, stumbling in their haste to reach the bedroom. Will had to stand aside to let them past. In the bedlam that followed a score of them tried to force their way into the small upstairs room while the others packed the landing, trying to get a glimpse of what was happening. No one paid any attention to the volunteer in the green jacket who flattened himself against the wall to let them go by.

Will could hear the thunder of feet upstairs and a man's voice, crying out in terror. A few moments later the mob emerged from the room, dragging a poor scared creature dressed only in a nightshirt. They frog-marched their prisoner downstairs, pinioning his arms so that his bare feet paddled the air. Will heard his voice bleating out above the din. "For pity's sake, don't hurt me! I'm English, I tell you! English!"

Eventually they set him down on a table, spread-eagled on his back. Faces brimming with contempt peered down at him. He cowered away from them like a dog that's about to be whipped, hiding his head in his hands. Arton Hughes prised one arm away and lowered his torch to get a better look at the prisoner's face.

"You fools!" he said, furiously. "This isn't him. It's only that fool Debney!"

"Then where's the Frenchman? Where did he go?" they demanded.

"He took my jacket!" said Debney, finding his tongue at last. "He put a pistol to my head and threatened to blow out my brains if I stirred from the bed. You must have passed him on the stairs!"

Too late, they remembered the fair-haired man in the green jacket who had stood on the landing and called down to them. In their haste to reach the bedroom they had brushed past, paying him no attention. Only Will and his mother had seen Louis slip silently behind the cellar door, while no one was looking. By now, Will thought, he would be deep in the tunnel that led under the West Hill.

7

The Letter

E arly the next morning Will took the coast path
that led to the lime kilns. The old ruins lay a
mile and a half to the west of the village, hidden in a
deep grassy valley that ran down to the sea. In the last
century the kilns had fallen into disuse and all that
was left now was a stone wall overgrown with ivy. An
arched door in the base of the wall led to the deep,
pot-shaped kiln inside where the lime was burnt.
Nowadays sheep grazed among the ruins and the only
sound was the lonely call of the gulls in the sky.

Will passed on by, leaving the path and climbing out
of the valley with the sea below him. A little further
on he turned north, picking his way over stony ground
until he reached a tall outcrop of grey rocks in the
hillside. The entrance to the cave was narrow, a dark

fissure where it was just possible to squeeze inside. Further on, Will knew the passage opened out to a much larger chamber, but the darkness of the entrance was enough to deter anyone but the brave from venturing deeper inside. Will had stumbled across the place one day when he had been out looking for gulls' eggs among the rocks.

He called Louis's name softly and heard a rustling from the back of the cave. The fugitive emerged looking pale and dishevelled, blinking in the bright morning light. He greeted Will warmly, shaking his hand. Will noticed he walked slightly bent over, and clutched at his side where his ribs still caused him pain.

Louis took him into the cave to show him where he had spent the night. On the floor was a rough bed of ferns and beside it a low fire filling the cave with swirling smoke that escaped along the passageway towards the entrance. Louis made light of his poor shelter, saying it was as good as some of the hovels that passed for houses in the poorer quarters of Paris.

Will had brought bread and cold bacon for breakfast and they ate it, sitting in the mouth of the cave where they could look down on the grey-green sea and hear the waves breaking gently against the foot of the cliff. Susannah had sent a bundle of clothes, including a brown woollen tailcoat which had once belonged to Will's father. It fitted Louis well enough, though it was a little broad across the shoulder. Will said he could easily pass for a farmer or a tradesman.

When the food was gone they talked for a while. Louis admitted that, after the events of the previous night, he had abandoned his plans to try and reach Brighton. He was an escaped prisoner now, and if the news had reached the garrison at Halston, perhaps the soldiers would be out looking for him already. He had little choice but to remain in hiding until he could find a boat to carry him back across the Channel to France. Will knew it wouldn't be easy. With the naval gunboats patrolling the coast, who would be willing to take the risk of helping a penniless Frenchman? When he left Louis they were no nearer to finding a solution. They parted outside the cave, and Will turned east towards the village with the pistol in his pocket that Louis had returned to him.

The day at school passed slowly. Will watched the clock on the wall behind Miss Parkes's head and his thoughts strayed to how Louis might be passing the time. He had warned him not to venture far from his hiding place in daylight.

After school, he caught sight of Hannah walking down the hill by herself. Something about the forlorn figure ahead of him made him forget his resolution to avoid her. He increased his pace, but before he could catch up with her, she was overtaken by two boys who seemed to be in a great hurry. Since Hannah's first day, Robert Newson had been waiting for an opportunity to take his revenge, but so far he had been frustrated. During school hours, he couldn't avoid Miss Parkes's vigilant eye, and at the end of the day, Hannah was often out of the gates and down the hill before the rest of the class had reached the yard.

Today however, Newson had spotted Hannah on her own and followed her down the street, in the company of Jack Merrit. Will saw Newson glance back over his shoulder, before turning into the narrow alley by the Customs House. This was Hannah's way home, winding along Salter's Lane and then cutting north towards the Rectory. It struck Will as odd that the two boys should choose the same route – he had never seen them take the alley before and Robert Newson lived in Three Post Lane at the bottom of the village. He saw Hannah turn into the narrow passage, apparently unaware that she had company.

Halting outside the door of the Customs House he wondered whether he should follow her or carry on down the hill, towards the Angel. As he was standing irresolute, he heard a shout from along the alley, a howl of rage that he recognized as Hannah's voice. Will ran down the passage and turned the bend in time to see her cornered by the two grinning boys where the alley opened into Salter's

Lane. Newson had a book in his hand, and something else, a piece of paper that might have been concealed in its pages.

"Give it back, you ape!" Hannah demanded. "Give it back or you'll be sorry!" Her face was white with fury and her hands were balled into two small fists. Newson ignored her and started to read the letter out loud in a mocking voice.

"My darling daughter, I pray you are. . ."

Hannah rushed at him but he was too quick for her and snatched the letter away. Jack Merrit caught her round the waist and held her tight, laughing at her attempts to break free. Newson held the letter by a corner, suspended over a puddle.

"If you want it, let's see you beg for it. On your knees!" he pointed to the puddle.

They were too occupied with their baiting of Hannah to pay Will any attention. There were two of them and Robert Newson was a handful on his own, big for his age and with a reputation for savagery. Yet Will couldn't find it in his heart to leave Hannah to face them alone. He ran at Newson with his head down and caught him in the chest with such force that the bigger boy was hurled on to the ground, into a heap of wet leaves under a beech tree. Will turned on Merrit, who still held Hannah round the waist, as if he was trying to hide behind her.

"Let her go!" ordered Will.

Merrit obeyed and flung Hannah to the ground with spiteful force. But his eyes darted to his left and Will turned in time to see Robert Newson back on his feet, advancing on him. Will was caught between them and knew that he couldn't fight them both at once. He backed away with his fists raised like a prize-fighter, until he found himself up against the wall of the alley, with no escape.

Behind them he caught sight of Hannah, on her hands and knees under the tree, apparently still worried about her precious letter. Will felt a sharp pang of irritation. He could have walked on by, but instead he had intervened to try and rescue her, yet she wasn't even interested in watching him put up a fight. Well, he would show her all the same. He would make sure he gave Newson something to remember him by. His opponents were closing in on him. Will determined he would try to stay on his feet as long as possible. He had seen Robert Newson kick a boy on the ground until his victim was as bruised as a fallen apple.

"Where you going to run now, pot-boy?" taunted Newson. He was red-faced, with his hair hanging over his eyes.

They both lunged for him at once, their heads down to avoid his wild punches. Will felt himself slammed up against the brick wall, the breath knocked out of him. He lashed out wildly, blindly, grazing his knuckles on bone and flesh. The next moment he heard a cry of anguish and Robert Newson staggered back.

Behind them, Hannah was holding the branch she had found among the dry leaves. It was as thick as a club and she had struck Robert Newson so hard across the shoulders that the end had broken off.

"Next time I'll break it over your thick skull," she warned. Newson and Merrit looked at each other. Her furious expression told them she wasn't joking. Hannah raised the branch higher and took a step closer to them, uttering a savage, ear-splitting cry.

Newson didn't wait to be hit again. The two of them took off down the alleyway as fast as they could run.

Will stood against the wall, panting for breath and staring dumbly at the slim girl in her white dress with the broken branch raised above her head.

"What's the matter?" she said. "Think I don't know how to fight? I've got two brothers at home and they're like little wildcats."

Will nodded. He doubted if Robert Newson would ever bother her at school again. He certainly wouldn't want the story to get around the schoolyard that he had run away from a girl.

Hannah dropped the branch on the ground and went back to crouch over the muddy puddle. She picked out her letter, which was crumpled and floating face-down. Will could see that the ink had run so that the words were little more than rows of smudges. Hannah held it tenderly, letting the dirty water drip down into the puddle, as if she thought the writing might form again by some magic.

"Was it from your parents?" asked Will.

"My mother," said Hannah. "It must have taken her hours to write. She never went to school. She had to learn her letters from me."

"Perhaps it can be dried over a candle," suggested Will.

Hannah shook her head. "It wouldn't be any use. I know it off by heart anyway. I've read it a thousand times." She stood up, brushed her dark hair out of her eyes, and looked at him curiously.

"Why did you stop to help me?"

Will shrugged. She was staring at him with her head on one side as if he was a puzzle. It made him feel awkward.

"All the others at school hate me. I've seen them whispering, the way they look at me."

She had begun walking up Salter's Lane in the direction of the Rectory and seemed to assume he was coming with her.

"It's not that they hate you," Will tried to explain. "It's just they need time to get used to you. You're not from our village. And you see, your uncle's the Rector."

"What difference does that make?"

"They think you're better than them, that you give yourself airs."

Hannah snorted in disbelief. "Me? Give myself my airs? You know why I've come to stay here with my uncle?"

Will shook his head.

"Because my family are too poor to keep me. My father's a pedlar who goes from house to house pushing his barrow. At least, that was his trade, before he fell ill. Now I'm living here on my uncle's charity, because at home there are too many mouths to feed and every penny goes to pay the doctor's bills. There, now you know the truth, tell them at school if you like so they can all laugh at me."

Her dark eyes were blazing defiance again. Will didn't know how to reply. Her mood seemed to switch from friendliness to hostility in a matter of seconds. They had reached the gates of the Rectory and he made as if to turn back down the hill, towards home. He was surprised when Hannah touched his arm lightly, and said. "Why don't you come in? I'm sure my uncle would like to meet you."

They both knew it was a lie, but there was a plea in her voice he couldn't ignore.

Will had never set foot inside the Rectory before. The Reverend Spencer kept it as his private sanctuary, confining his brief exchanges with his flock to the church door after Matins or Evensong. Sitting in the dining room at the large table, with his hands clasping a china teacup, Will looked around him. The walls were oak-panelled and hung with pictures of dreary landscapes in faded greens and browns. A mantel clock ticked above the fireplace, cold and empty, as the Rector didn't allow a fire until the evening. Apart from the table and chairs, the room was sparsely furnished. The Reverend Spencer sipped his tea and peered at Will over the rim of the cup. He had lank silver-grey hair and a long goatish face. His eyes, small and sharp, emerged from a pool of wrinkles. He cleared his throat.

"So. My niece tells me you live at the Angel Inn."

"Yes sir, with my mother. She's the landlady," said Will.

"Mrs Finch, I believe."

"Yes, sir."

"And your father? I don't believe we have ever seen him in church?"

Will looked down awkwardly at the cup in his hands. "My father died when I was four."

"Indeed. I am sorry to hear it," said the Reverend. He attempted a smile, drawing his thin lips together, but there was no spark of warmth in his eyes. Will glanced at Hannah, who had put down her cup and seemed to be waiting for the moment when they could escape from the table. When they had first sat down she had seemed in high spirits, telling her uncle a watered-down version of their adventure on the way home from school. But gradually, under the disapproving gaze of the Reverend Spencer, she had lapsed into silence, leaving Will to cope alone with her uncle's polite interrogation.

Will tried to imagine her living in this dark silent house with its long passageways and cold rooms, and only her severe uncle for company. He imagined Hannah and the Rector sitting down to supper, with the mantel clock ticking and their spoons scraping their bowls. Perhaps her uncle sometimes brought a book of sermons to read at the table. It was so unlike his own home, where Will often ate his supper in a hurry, standing up in the kitchen, with his mother bustling in and out and the noise of talk and laughter spilling through the door from the parlour. The Rectory was much grander than the Angel Inn, but it reflected the gloominess of its owner. It was no wonder, Will thought, that Hannah seemed so unhappy at school. He guessed that her life had been unbearably lonely since she'd come to Lydwell, that she pored over her mother's letter because it provided her one link with home.

"No doubt my niece has told you the unfortunate news about her father," the Reverend Spencer was saying, and Will realized he was being addressed.

"Oh yes, sir," he said. "That is, she told me he is ill, and I'm very sorry to hear it."

Hannah shot him a grateful smile.

"And did she tell you that she wishes, she *desires* to visit her family? She considers it a matter of urgency."

Will glanced at Hannah. "No sir. But if he is ill. . ."

"*Gravely* ill, if we can believe my sister's letter, though the spelling would do no credit to a child."

Hannah leaned forward eagerly. "Then you'll let me go, Uncle? Tomorrow? You said you would consider it."

The Reverend sighed and brought the palms of his hands together under his chin – a gesture he often used in his sermons. "It is a three-hour journey to Crowhurst from here, and the roads are dangerous. There are footpads, perhaps even highwaymen. Your father is ill and you wish to see him, Hannah, that is understandable and does you credit, but as your guardian I must forbid such a journey. If something were to happen to you, I would be to blame. No, I fear it would be unwise, most unwise."

Hannah's face had fallen, but just as quickly it brightened with hope.

"Then come with me, Uncle! We could journey together, the two of us, so you'd be sure I was safe."

The Reverend shook his head. "Alas, child, as I told you, there are matters here I must attend to. Nothing would give me greater pleasure than to bring some comfort to your poor father but I fear it is impossible, quite impossible. And besides, your mother's letter speaks of this infernal man Moses again."

"Moses?" said Will. He had never heard the name before.

"That is what he calls himself," said Hannah with a bitter laugh. "He leads a gang of smugglers who are the plague of the marshes."

Will shifted in his seat uncomfortably at the mention of smugglers. Hannah knew nothing of what went on in the village after dark.

"All of which proves my point," said the Reverend. "It would be dangerous for you to go home at present. With this man Moses still at large, you are safer here, well away from Crowhurst. That is why your mother sent you away in the first place, Hannah. Now the matter is closed, let us say no more about it."

The Reverend Spencer rose from the table, but Hannah left her seat and intercepted him at the door, clinging to his arm.

"Please, Uncle, I've never asked you for anything else. I only wish to see my father this once – before it is too late. I do not care if the journey is long, just give me your permission to go. Please." There were tears in her eyes and the plea would have melted a heart of stone. But the Reverend Spencer prided himself that he never let his heart rule his head. Will saw him hesitate and withdraw his hand stiffly. Before he knew it, he heard his own voice speak up.

"Perhaps if I went with Hannah, sir, that would set your mind at ease."

The Reverend looked at him in surprise. "*You?* You go with her?"

"Yes, sir. People would take us for brother and sister, we look much alike. I would promise to take good care of her and we would be back by the following morning."

"Well," said the Reverend, "it is true I would feel happier if Hannah had a travelling companion. But you're no more than a youth yourself. . ."

"I'm thirteen," said Will. "And I have travelled by myself on the stagecoach before without coming to any harm – to visit my aunt in Winchelsea."

"Is that so?" The Reverend sighed deeply and glanced at Hannah, waiting anxiously for his verdict. The girl was headstrong and would never give him any peace. Besides, no one could say he hadn't tried to dissuade her. "You would need your mother's permission," he said to Will.

Hannah settled the matter by standing on tiptoe to kiss him on the cheek. "Thank you, Uncle, you won't regret it. Thank you."

When it was time to go she came with Will to the gate.

"Have you really travelled on the stagecoach before?" she asked.

"Never," grinned Will. "But I've always wanted to."

8

Village in the Marsh

The stagecoach would set off from Lydwell at seven on Saturday morning, taking the turnpike road into Kent. Will had never travelled so far from home before, and hadn't been in a coach, so he looked forward to the journey as a great adventure. At first he'd worried that his mother might refuse him permission to go, but it didn't prove difficult to persuade her. He could tell that his mother was flattered and surprised that Will should be asked to accompany the Rector's niece as her companion. For once, she said, she could manage the inn by herself.

The day dawned damp and cold and Will shivered as he climbed up on to the top of the stagecoach outside the Swan Inn. They would be travelling "on the outside" since the fare for this was only two shillings, half as much as a seat in the coach. While the Reverend Spencer was willing to pay for his niece to travel in comfort, he felt that a seat on the roof would serve Will just as well. Hannah, however, had insisted that she wanted to travel on top, where she could breathe the air and pass the journey talking to "her dear brother". Will didn't bother to argue. He was learning that once Hannah had made up her mind, she seldom gave way.

The coach was soon rattling on its way, rocking from side to side and leaving clouds of dust in its wake. Overhead the sky was an iron grey and all that Will could glimpse of the landscape was bare trees rushing by and the fields beyond stretching away towards the sea. Hannah was seated next to the coachman, a burly, stern-faced man swaddled in a coat with a great number of capes. He wielded a long whip that every now and then he cracked in the air above the heads of the horses. Behind the driver's box, Will hung on as best as he could with the other passengers. His legs hung over the side and with every lurch on the muddy, uneven road he felt his bones shaken, and worried he would lose his grip and fall under the great wooden wheels spinning below him. For a long time the rolling of the coach made him feel sick and his mood didn't improve when Hannah turned round in her seat and laughed at his white face and wretched expression.

Once they'd stopped at a coaching inn and he had some bread and warm coffee inside his queasy stomach, he felt a little better. As they travelled on, the landscape began to alter as they crossed the border into Kent and entered the marshlands west of Romney. Will had heard travellers talk about the marshes, but he had never imagined a place could be so bleak or alien. For miles around all he could see was the flat brown marsh divided by the narrow dykes that criss-crossed the land. The sky was so vast and unending that it looked as if would crush the earth beneath it. Dotted here and there were isolated farms and dismal ponds fringed with tall reeds. Everything was clothed in the damp mist that seemed to cling to the land like white lace. Will hunched his shoulders against the wind and felt the chill of the place seeping into his bones. As mile after mile of the same landscape passed by, he longed for the sight of a steep hill or a rolling valley. Eventually Hannah pointed to a church tower, half a mile distant.

"There it is!" she said.

The driver turned to look at her. He hadn't spoken a word on the journey but now he broke his silence.

"Pardon me, Miss, but you surely don't mean Crowhurst?"

"I live there," replied Hannah. "I was born in the village."

"God almighty!" said the driver and shook his

head, cracking his whip at the horses as if he blamed them for bringing him to such a desolate place. As the coach swung into the village, he spoke again. "I can take you on as far as Romney, Miss," he offered. "You'll find good lodging at the Anchor and you'll be warm and safe there. If you'll take my advice, you'll not stop here the night. They say the village is cursed."

Hannah thanked him but explained they had come to visit her father and wished to be collected in the morning for the journey home. The coachman made no answer but pulled on the reins to bring the horses to a halt outside an inn called the Eagle and Child. Even as they climbed down, he had collected their bags and thrown them from the basket on to the ground. They watched as he urged the horses forward and the stagecoach turned south towards the coast road, disappearing out of sight with the passengers still clinging to the roof.

The village was much like the others they'd passed, with one inn, a church facing on to a green, and a sprinkling of poor cottages. As they walked through it, Will was struck by the silence, which after the continuous rattle and clatter of the coach on the road seemed strange and uncanny. Though it was now past ten o'clock in the morning, few of the villagers were stirring. Once, they saw some young children playing with a bat and ball in the lane, but as they drew nearer the mother appeared and took them by the hand, pulling them inside and closing the door behind them. Will began to wonder if the village was largely abandoned, until they met an old woman crossing the lane to her house from the churchyard.

"Mrs Moffat!" Hannah called out.

The old woman turned round, startled, and seemed about to hurry away into her house, until Hannah ran and caught up with her.

"It's me, Mrs Moffat, Hannah! You surely haven't forgotten me so soon?"

The old woman peered at Hannah more closely, reaching out a wrinkled hand to her cheek.

"Well, Lord bless us, Hannah! I thought you was in Sussex with your uncle."

"I was," said Hannah. "But I've come home to see my father. This is my friend, Will."

The old woman's gaze travelled over Will's face before returning to Hannah. "You'll find your father worse," she said. "And what with the way things are, maybe he's lost the will to go on." She looked up and down the street and lowered her voice almost to a whisper. "*He* has been back since you went. Twice he's been here with his band of devils."

"Moses?" said Hannah.

"Aye, Moses Morley. Burning Moses we call him," said the old woman addressing Will, "because he comes with fire and sets the thatch of your roof ablaze. That's what happened in Hornchurch, and a whole family perished in one night. Five children, they say, and Moses and his men stood outside listening to their screams and watching the smoke rise higher. He is the devil, I tell you, boy, Lucifer himself."

"What about the Revenue?" asked Will. "Why don't they arrest him?"

"The Revenue? Lord bless you, boy, this is the marshes, they don't dare come here! They are too mortal scared. But there, I've said too much already. Go in and see your mother, Hannah. You should not have come back, but stay indoors tonight and bolt the door. If you hear horses, snuff out the candle and don't go near the window. Pray he'll pass by, that's what we all do, turn to the wall and pray."

With this ominous piece of advice, the old woman pulled her shawl around her and disappeared into her house. Will and Hannah went on in silence to the end of the village where Hannah's house stood at a bend in the lane. Like the others it was a low plaster and timber cottage with diamond-pane windows and a garden where a vegetable patch was losing its battle against a tangle of weeds.

Hannah's mother was sitting at a table with her back to them when they entered. She turned round and Will saw a short, ample woman with dark hair like Hannah's that escaped from her day cap and got in her eyes. Her face lit up in wonder when she saw her daughter and for a moment she looked as if she thought she was dreaming.

"Well, Mother?" said Hannah. "Don't you have a kiss for me?"

Will stood by as Hannah was hugged and held and kissed. Her two small brothers came running and threw themselves upon her with cries of delight. Hannah introduced them as Joshua and Jeremiah. They stared at Will shyly and clung around their sister.

"But here we all are standing a-talking, and you haven't seen your father yet!" exclaimed Mrs Burrell. "It will be a treat for him, pick him up no end it will. See, Ned, who has come all this way to see you by the coach, and bringing her friend as well!"

She drew aside a piece of calico that had been hung from a beam as a makeshift curtain and behind it they found Hannah's father lying in bed. His skin had a greyish hue like old parchment and the bones of his cheeks almost seemed to show through. His chest rose and fell as his breathing came in shallow gasps that were painful even to witness. Will thought that each time he took a breath it might be his last. His whole body was bathed in sweat and a stale, sweet odour clung to his nightshirt. Will could see from Hannah's face that she was shocked at her father's weakened condition, though she tried not to show it. She sat down on the bed and stroked his hand, speaking to him softly like a child.

"See how he smiles up at you!" said Mrs Burrell, positively beaming. "I think he looks better already. The doctor bled him on Wednesday and I'm sure it's done him a power of good. . ."

Will felt he should leave Hannah with her father and slipped out from behind the curtain. The cottage had only the one downstairs room, paved with brick and divided by a partition. On shelves and cupboards there was evidence of Mr Burrell's former trade – cambric for handkerchiefs and yards of muslin and cotton. In one corner there was a handsome clock case, but no sound came from it and when Will opened the door, the workings were missing, perhaps sold off to pay a debt. Will looked down to find one of Hannah's brothers, Jeremiah, staring up at him with wide brown eyes. The boy must have been five or six years old.

"Will you play with me?" he asked solemnly.

"All right," said Will, squatting down to the boy's level. "What shall we play?"

"Smugglers," replied the boy. "You must hide in your bed and stay very quiet. Then I will come to get you."

After a simple meal of potatoes and cabbage they stayed up talking. But as the dark closed in outside, Will noticed that Mrs Burrell only half listened to the conversation. Now and then she glanced out of the window and listened for any sound on the road outside. When the church clock chimed nine, she said they must be tired from their long journey and would want to go to bed. Will took his candle upstairs to the front bedroom, where he found Hannah's two brothers already asleep in the bed. Jeremiah was lying on his side, with his cheek nuzzled against his brother's shoulder. Will wondered why they had not been sent away from the village like their sister, but perhaps their mother could not bear to be parted from them. Blowing out the candle, he squeezed under the covers nudging Jeremiah over to make room.

Outside, the village was silent and if he shut his eyes he could imagine he was back home, safe in his bedroom at the Angel. He thought about the man called Moses and wondered what kind of a smuggler could rule a whole village and keep its residents in a state of perpetual fear. When he had asked about Moses Morley over supper, Mrs Burrell had looked at him with pleading eyes and shaken her head, but the two boys had heard the name and stared at him as if he had uttered a blasphemy. Tomorrow, in any case, he would be heading home on the coach, and would be glad to leave Crowhurst behind. He burrowed under the thin blanket, hoping that sleep would come quickly, and with it the morning.

9

Burning Moses

When he awoke the room was folded in darkness and it was the dead of night. For a moment Will couldn't remember how he came to be in this strange, earthy-smelling room, but then his hand brushed against Jeremiah's small warm body in the bed beside him and it came back to him; this was Hannah's house and she was asleep in the back room with her mother. Outside a dog barked somewhere in the village. Will tried to surrender himself to sleep once more but when it came he was troubled by disturbing dreams. Once he thought he heard horses on the road, but he wasn't sure if it was real or part of his nightmare. From across the landing a floorboard creaked, and he heard light footsteps moving around. A moment later Hannah stole into the room barefooted, holding a candle thrust ahead of her so that she cast a giant shadow on the wall. She was dressed in her white nightgown with her hair loose. Putting a finger to her lips, she went to the window without a word. Will crept out of bed, trying not to wake the two young boys, who were still sleeping peacefully. Standing beside Hannah, he peered into the dark outside, straining every nerve to listen.

At first he could see nothing but blackness and dared to hope that Hannah had imagined whatever had woken her. Then he caught sight of a light at the other end of the village, joined by others until there were a dozen yellow eyes moving towards them. Hannah blew out the candle and he felt her hand reach up instinctively and grip his arm.

"Heaven help us, it is him, Will," she whispered. "It is Moses."

He had never known her scared before, and her fear began to infect him. He had met smugglers before and knew each of them in Lydwell by name, but by all accounts these marsh smugglers were another breed. They were murderers. They had set fire to a house and stood by while the women and children inside were burned alive. They didn't fear the law or the Revenue; the marsh was their kingdom and here they ruled by terror.

Shadows moved in the dark and Will saw a man go to a door and heard him beat on it with his fists. When the door was eventually opened, sharp words were exchanged and after a minute, the owner was dragged outside into the street. Will saw now that everywhere the same story was being repeated – the men of the village were being driven from their homes and herded together like sheep on the green in front of the church.

"Where are they taking them?" Will whispered.

"To the coast. They are Moses's packhorses," Hannah replied. "They're to carry the cargo on their backs across the marsh. If they come to the door, don't open it. If we stay quiet, perhaps they'll think the house is empty and pass on."

"What if they don't?"

"They'll take you too, if they find you here. They take whomever they please. Even women sometimes."

Even as she spoke, there came a hammering at the door below them that would have woken the dead. They both drew back away from the window and crouched in the dark by the wall, listening to the insistent pounding and the voices demanding they open up.

Then another voice reached them from the room below, a high whimpering moan that sounded like a frightened child.

Hannah caught her breath. "Father! I must go down or they'll hear him. Stay with the boys."

She left him and plunged off into the darkness. He heard her bare feet pattering downstairs. Will wanted to go with her, but now Jeremiah was awake and was sitting up in bed, plainly terrified by the noise from below. He started to cry, calling out for his mother. Will crawled on to the bed beside him and wrapped his arms around the boy, stifling his sobs against his chest. "It's all right, it's all right," he whispered, over and over again, unable to think of any other words to comfort the boy.

For a moment there was an unexpected silence downstairs. The beating on the door ceased and Ned Burrell stopped his fevered moaning. Then there was a deafening crash as the door was kicked in. Will could hear screams from Hannah's mother, who at that moment must have been stealing quietly down the stairs. The next moments were filled with a confusion of noise so that he couldn't tell what was happening below. He wanted to rush down the stairs, but both the brothers were awake now and clung to him, begging him not to leave them.

Finally he heard what sounded like someone being dragged across the room, followed by the wails of Hannah's mother. "For pity's sake, can't you see he is sick? You'll kill him! You'll kill him!" Her voice ended in a howl of despair and anguish. Will could bear to listen no longer and struggled free from the grasp of the two terrified boys.

"Stay there," he said to them. "Stay there and whatever happens, don't leave this room."

"Are they going to kill our father?" asked Jeremiah.

"No, no. Stay there and I will send Hannah!"

They nodded at him dumbly and clung to each other in the dark, two small shapes huddled in the corner of the bed.

Downstairs Will found a scene of chaos, with the curtain lying on the floor, the bed empty and the door leaning at a strange angle. Hannah was outside, trying to comfort her distraught mother.

"They've taken him," she told Will. "I begged them, but they wouldn't listen!"

Will told her to look after her brothers and ran out into the road. All was in chaos, with the street full of horses and men going back and forth. He dodged in and out of them until he caught sight of Hannah's father among the group of men who had been herded together on the grass in front of the church. Some of the villagers had managed to bring their coats, hats and boots, knowing that ahead of them lay a long cold trudge across the marshes to the sea. But Ned Burrell was dressed only in his thin nightshirt and was down on his hands and knees in the damp grass, as if he was searching for something. Before Will could reach him, one of the smugglers stepped forward and gave Hannah's father a violent kick in the ribs.

"On your feet, you old fool!" he ordered. "What are you? A dog crawling on your belly?"

Will helped Ned Burrell to his feet. Despite the cold of the night, his face was clammy with sweat and deathly white. He was shivering and struggling to catch his breath from the violent blow he'd just received.

Will addressed the man who had kicked him. "Can't you see this man is sick? He has the fever!"

"I care not if he's as mad as the moon, if he has two arms and legs then he comes with us. Them's the captain's orders and I don't argue with them. If you know what's good for you, you'll pipe down and do what you're told."

"Look at him!" pleaded Will. "He can hardly stand by himself. He would never make it across the marsh. He has the fever, I tell you, the *fever*!"

Will found he had almost shouted the word and was aware of the villagers behind them, drawing back in alarm. They had heard there was fever in the Burrells' house. None of them had been near it these last two weeks. The smuggler looked closely at Ned Burrell's face in the light of his torch and promptly took a step back.

"The devil! Why didn't you say so before?" He turned and called to a man nearby who sat astride a tall chestnut horse, waiting impatiently.

"Captain, there's one here you better take a look at."

As the man turned his horse towards them, Will got his first glimpse of the one the villagers called Moses.

He was powerfully built with a barrel chest and a bull neck. It was the frame of a boxer or a blacksmith. "What is the delay, Stubbs?" he said. "I told you to have them ready to march."

"The boy here says the old fellow has the fever," said the one called Stubbs. "I don't like the smell of him myself, he stinks like an open grave. Say the word and we'll leave him behind."

Moses dismounted and took the torch from Stubbs's hand. He brought it close to Ned Burrell's face to get a better look at him. Hannah's father shrank away from the flames in alarm. Up close, Will saw that Morley's skin was pitted and scarred with the marks of smallpox. His face was a ruin but his black eyes burned with malevolence.

"Fever, you say? He looks well enough to me," he said. "Perhaps he is malingering?"

"No, truthfully, sir," said Will. "He has had the fever these two weeks and is as weak as a child. Let me take his place. . ."

"Hold your peace!" roared Moses in sudden fury. "You dare tell me what to do, boy? Who I shall take and who leave behind?" Without warning, he pulled one of the pistols from his belt and pointed the muzzle at the head of poor Ned Burrell. "Perhaps I should blow out his brains now and put an end to his miserable life, what do you say to that?"

Mr Burrell's eyes bulged with terror and the

sweat shone on his rosy face. He shook his head helplessly.

"No? You want to live, old man? Then prove you can be some use. There is my horse, go and fetch my saddle and bring it over here." Hannah's father stared back at his tormentor, fear and confusion mingled in his expression.

"You heard me, you old fool!" thundered Morley. "Bring me the saddle or I pull the trigger."

"He cannot, sir!" pleaded Will.

"Silence!" roared Moses. "Let him go."

Will had no choice. If he tried to intervene, he would only whip Morley into a greater fury. He saw now he was dealing with a madman who would kill on the slightest provocation. He removed Ned Burrell's arm from round his shoulder and watched him take a step forward. The distance to the mare with the saddle on its back was only fifteen paces, but for Hannah's father it might as well have been a mile. The smugglers had gathered round in a knot to watch the sport and began to laugh as he took another faltering step towards the horse.

"I'll wager a guinea he doesn't reach it!" called out Stubbs. Will glanced up at Hannah's house and thought he caught sight of someone at the front bedroom window. He hoped that she wasn't watching her father's humiliation. Five, six more steps and Ned Burrell wavered and fell to his knees, but he tottered back to his feet, as if he knew his life depended on completing this simple task. From somewhere he seemed to find new reserves of strength and covered the rest of the ground, clinging on to the horse while he panted with effort.

"Now for the saddle, old man," said Moses. "Unbuckle it and bring it here to me."

Hannah's father struggled with the buckles of the girth, fumbling in his haste. Eventually he was able to wrench the saddle free, but it was too heavy for his failing strength and it slid off the horse, thudding to the ground. He tried to pick it up and managed to drag it four or five steps, before falling once again. He was still ten steps away from reaching his goal, but it was clear he had exhausted himself. When Moses came to stand over him he raised his head, looking up at his executioner like a dumb animal. The smugglers had ceased their laughter, waiting to see if the poor wretch on the ground was going to die.

"Well, I believe you, old man, you have the fever," said Moses. "I see now you are burning up."

How it happened Will didn't see, but the next instant the flames from the torch in Moses' hand had spread to the hem of Ned Burrell's nightshirt and he was writhing and screaming, beating at the flames round his legs like a man possessed. Moses had taken a step back and was laughing wildly with his scarred ugly face thrown back.

For a moment Will was paralysed by the horror of

the spectacle, then he rushed forward and grabbed Hannah's father, rolling him over and over in the damp grass, until the flames had been smothered. Ned Burrell lay moaning with his face pressed to the earth. Will turned to look at the maniac responsible, but Moses had already lost interest and was lifting his saddle back on to his horse.

"What shall we do with him?" asked Stubbs.

"Leave him," said Moses, indifferently. "We've work to do and we've wasted enough time here already. Get them moving and make sure the boy does his share of the work. We are one man short tonight, and he will have to make good the loss."

The journey across the marshes that night felt like the longest of Will's life. Will didn't know how many miles they walked before they reached the sea – all he remembered was trudging endlessly through the marshes and crossing dykes where the brackish water rose over his boots, his feet numb with cold. His companions from Crowhurst and the neighbouring villages trudged beside him, never speaking a word all the way. They marched in a ragged line with Moses riding at the head of them like a merchant bringing his slaves to market. The smugglers rode on horses, with the one called Stubbs trotting ahead of the prisoners and another at their back urging them on with savage threats. If anyone stumbled or showed signs of lagging behind, one of the smugglers would lean down from his horse and strike them across the back with his whip. In this way they reached the sea, where a smuggling vessel lay waiting – a lugger painted black as night – and Will saw the blue flare against the sky as the signal was passed from the shore.

When Will finally returned to the village that night, muddy, exhausted and chilled to the bone, he found a lamp burning in the parlour and Hannah waiting up for him. She was fast asleep in an armchair with a blanket drawn over her. The curtain had been hung back in its place in the corner, and behind it Will could hear the rasping sound of Ned Burrell's breathing. Despite the terrors he had suffered that night, Hannah's father had evidently survived. Will reflected that to live another day in this tormented place could hardly be counted a blessing.

10

A Glint of Gold

The next morning, soon after nine o'clock, the coach pulled into the village to take them back to Lydwell. Hannah found it a painful wrench to be parted from her family again, especially after what she had witnessed the previous night. But despite all her protests, Mrs Burrell would not hear of her daughter staying.

"It will be a great comfort to me," she said, "to think of you safe and well in your uncle's fine house at Lydwell. As for your father, you mustn't worry, Hannah, I'm sure that the worst of the fever is passed and he is on the mend. Dr Parry will come and see him tomorrow. And as soon as he is up and on his pegs again, I will write and send for you."

Will could tell that Hannah did not share her

mother's optimism – this morning he had heard Ned Burrell muttering to himself in a delirium that was somewhere between sleep and waking. The encounter with Morley had left its mark both on his mind and his body. His legs were badly burned and in the night Will had heard him crying for help, convinced that the smugglers were coming back for him. Hannah had stayed at his bedside trying to soothe him until it was time to go. When finally she climbed on to the box-seat and the coachman cracked his whip, she kept waving to her family until the coach had rounded the bend and passed out of sight.

The further they travelled from her home, the more she sunk into despondency, and Will felt a little guilty that his own mood lifted as soon as they left the marshes behind. As they neared the border of Sussex, his thoughts returned to his own concerns and the question of what to do about Louis. It was possible that Lieutenant Lock had abandoned the search for the escaped Frenchman by now, but Will doubted it. Lock was a man with a high opinion of himself and he would certainly feel his reputation had been damaged by letting an important prisoner slip through his fingers. Will wondered if Louis was safe and how he had survived in his absence. There hadn't been time to warn his friend that he would be gone from the village for a day and a night.

When they reached Lydwell, he walked with

Hannah as far as the gate of her uncle's house. It was just after midday but there was no sign of life from the Rectory. The grey stone house looked as austere and forbidding as ever and Will understood why Hannah preferred her parents' untidy cottage in Crowhurst, despite the shadow that lay over the village. Now as they stood at the gate, he hesitated. There was something he wanted to tell her.

"You remember the night of the shipwreck?" he said.

"Of course. It was the night after I came here."

"And the man we rescued?"

"I was right, wasn't I?" said Hannah. "He was French. My uncle says he's escaped and now there's talk of a reward for anyone who finds him. The soldiers are out looking."

"Which soldiers?" said Will.

"I don't know, from the garrison, I suppose."

"Did your uncle say where they are they looking? Try and remember, Hannah, it's important. . ."

He broke off. She was looking at him strangely, struck by a sudden intuition. "You know where he is, don't you?" she said. "You know where he's hiding!"

Will nodded.

Hannah stared at him open-mouthed. "Why didn't you tell me before?"

"I couldn't," said Will. "Not until I was sure I could trust you. If he's found they'll throw him into prison,

Hannah. Perhaps even hang him. All he wants is to return home to his family. And he's done nothing wrong, nothing at all."

"My uncle says he's a spy," said Hannah. "That's what the talk is in the village."

"People believe what they want," said Will bitterly. "They know nothing about him."

"Where is he now?" asked Hannah.

Will glanced back along the lane to make sure no one was coming. "You have to promise," he said. "Promise you'll never breathe a word of this to anyone."

"I won't," said Hannah. "If you believe he's innocent, then so do I."

He told her then about Louis and how he had escaped from the inn disguised in James Debney's uniform (though he said nothing of the secret passage leading from the Angel's cellar). He told her about the cave beyond the lime kilns where Louis was hiding, waiting to find a ship that would take him back to France. And Hannah listened to it all with her eyes shining, as if it was a great adventure in which she was being asked to play a part. When Will revealed that he planned to visit Louis that same afternoon, she begged him to take her along so that she could see the cave and meet the fugitive herself. He agreed readily. Up to now, the only other person who knew about Louis was Susannah, and Will knew his mother disapproved of his secret visits to the lime kilns. The penalty for anyone caught helping an escaped prisoner of war would be severe. It was somehow a relief to explain it all to Hannah, so that he didn't have to carry the burden of his secret all alone. They arranged to meet at the foot of the coast path later that afternoon, when both of them had eaten and rested from the journey.

It was late afternoon when they finally reached the lime kilns. The sun was already low in the sky, obscured by a dark curtain of clouds drifting in from the west. It parted for a moment and a shaft of light touched the tops of the cliffs with gold. Will regretted that they hadn't set out earlier, remembering the sky had looked just as ominous on the night of the storm, when the *Fortune* had struck the reef. He was glad that he'd brought one of the two brass lanterns from the snug. Hannah had a basket over her arm, containing a few provisions that she had stolen from her uncle's pantry when Mrs Lawson was cleaning the house upstairs. To anyone else, Hannah said, they would look like two children out looking for blackberries along the cliffs.

Yet, when they reached the cave and squeezed through the narrow entrance, they found it empty. There was Louis's bed of ferns and the cold ashes of a fire, but there was no sign of the cave's occupant. Will hoped Louis couldn't be far away. Surely he would know that the soldiers would be combing the coast, looking for him? The musket and pistol that he had taken from Debney were also missing, which at least meant that he was armed.

They waited in the cave for almost an hour, but when no one came, Hannah grew impatient and said they should leave the food and look along the cliff path. It was growing dark by the time they emerged. The sun had sunk below the rim of the horizon and the wind whipped their hair into their eyes and tugged at the branches of the trees. Will glanced up at the sky, where the clouds were gathering like ravens, and wondered if it would be wiser to turn back, but Hannah was already pressing on ahead of him, climbing back towards the path. They followed the coast west for a mile, past Stairhole Cove, but saw no sign of Louis.

When the rain came it was as if a window in the sky had been opened. Before long their clothes were sodden and they were forced to abandon the path, running downhill into a tree-lined valley to seek shelter. They found themselves in a wood of gnarled oaks and sycamores, where wild garlic filled the air with its heavy pungent scent. The rain dripped from the branches overhead as they tried to shelter under an ancient oak, bare of leaves. Hannah pointed to a gap in the trees, where the top of a chimney was visible.

"There's a cottage. We could ask for shelter," she said. "Perhaps they'll have a fire or will offer us something to eat." Normally Will wouldn't have called at a stranger's house outside the village, but he was shivering with cold and the prospect of drying out in front of a warming fire was too good to resist.

When they reached the house, however, their hopes were dashed. It was an abandoned hovel. No smoke issued from the chimney and it looked as if no one had lived there for years. Will tried to peer through one of the two small casement windows at the front, rubbing away the dust and grime with his fingers. It was too dark to see anything inside.

"Empty," he said, disappointed. Nevertheless Hannah rapped loudly on the door just to make sure. In answer they heard a thump from within, which startled them so much that Hannah jumped back from the door in alarm. Rapid footsteps crossed the floor inside and a door banged at the back of the cottage. For a minute they stood rooted to the spot, uncertain what to do. Will signalled to Hannah to remain where she was and made his way stealthily along the side of the house. At the back he found a yard with an empty pigsty, but no sign of life. A door gaped open. Whoever they had surprised had disappeared into the woods, running away like a startled deer.

When he returned to the front door he found Hannah gone and followed her inside. The house was full of shadows, smelling of damp earth and the neglect of years. The rain drummed on the roof and occasional drips came down the chimney, splashing softly in the fireplace. In the middle of the room was a long oak table and two benches. The doors of a dresser lay open and there were pewter bowls and pans strewn across the floor. Everything was covered in a fine layer of dust.

Will instinctively kept his voice low. "We shouldn't be here," he said. "What if they come back?"

Hannah brushed a cobweb from a window. "No one has lived here for years. In any case, they won't mind if we make a fire. My clothes are wet through."

She walked towards the hearth, but halted halfway across the room. Her hand flew to her mouth and Will saw she was staring at something beyond the table with a look of horror.

"What is it?" he asked.

In the near-darkness of the cottage they hadn't noticed the body on the floor. The dead man lay on his side, his torso twisted unnaturally, with one arm trapped underneath him and the other reaching out. For a long time neither of them dared to go any closer. Will had seen a body before, in the back room of Liney Roach's house, laid out ready for burial, but this one still retained the recent bloom of life. He could see the dark hole in the forehead where the ball had entered. A thin ribbon of blood trickled into the man's brown hair. On the floor nearby was the pistol he had dropped or had been trying to reach when he was shot.

Will stood by while Hannah knelt down beside the body to study the dead man's face.

"Do you know him?" she asked.

Will shook his head. "He's not from the village. We should get away from here, Hannah."

Neither of them moved.

"There's something in his hand." Hannah turned over the hand that was caught under the body and unfurled the tightly clasped fingers. Inside there was something small and bright. The glitter of gold made her catch her breath.

"A golden guinea," she said in wonder and held it up for Will to see.

"Put it back. We have to leave," said Will. His voice was urgent. "Hannah, listen to me. Whoever did this may be coming back."

But she wasn't listening. She stood up and brought the coin into the light of the lamp that stood on the table, examining it as if it would reveal its secrets.

"Why was he holding a guinea?" she asked. "You don't see them so often."

"I don't know, Hannah. Please!"

She was looking around, deaf to his words, too

absorbed in trying to piece together the evidence of the room. "There was an argument," she said. "A fight. He drew his pistol from his belt, but the other one must have been quicker. But what were they fighting over?"

Will made a despairing gesture. He didn't know and it wasn't the time to ask questions. They should go while there was still time. The man they had disturbed, who had run off, must have been the murderer. What if even now he was watching the house, or waiting outside for them?

"They were looking for something!" Hannah said, breaking into his thoughts. She gestured at the evidence of the ransacked room: the doors of the dresser hanging open, the drawers pulled out and pans strewn across the floor, as if someone had been searching desperately, in a great hurry.

"For what?" said Will.

"I don't know, something important, but we interrupted them. Help me look!"

"No, Hannah!"

"Then I'll look myself."

She crossed to the fireplace, reaching up inside the chimney breast to feel for anything that might be concealed there. Will began to help search the house, half-heartedly, just so that she would agree to leave – listening all the time for the approach of anyone outside. He climbed the stairs but found nothing besides an empty room where the floorboards creaked beneath his feet and dead flies had collected on the window ledge. When he came back down, Hannah had dragged one end of the cupboard away from the wall and was looking behind it.

"Come on!" he said impatiently. "We've seen enough. There's nothing here."

"All right, I'm coming. What about this?" she held up the golden guinea between her thumb and forefinger.

"Leave it!" He knocked the coin out of her hand angrily. It hit the flagstones and spun on its side across the floor, performing an arc until abruptly it vanished from sight.

"Why did you do that? You've lost it." Hannah sank down on her knees and examined the floor with the lamp. "Will, look at this!" Her voice was excited. Will knelt down beside her, curious in spite of himself. In the dim light of the lamp he could see a gap in the floor, running the length of one of the flagstones. It was hardly more than a crack, but the guinea must have slipped down it and disappeared without a trace. Even he had to admit it was strange. He pushed his fingers into the crack and found that the flagstone beside it was loose. It came up without resistance as if it was designed for that very purpose. The stone was heavy but between the two of them they were able to drag it clear. Beneath they found a square wooden frame that had supported the flagstone and under that, a dark hole which went down three or four feet. Will had seen tub-holes before; they were used to conceal a barrel of spirits from the Customs men – and this hole might certainly have been designed for the same purpose – but there was no barrel inside. Instead a foul musky smell reached them from the dark below.

Hannah thrust her lamp into the dark. "There's something down there. See if you can reach it."

Will shot her a look. Why did it have to be him? He lay down beside the hole and thrust his arm into it up to his shoulder. His fingertips scraped earth at the bottom.

"Well?" she asked impatiently.

"Ugh!" Will's fingers brushed against something soft and sleek. He drew his hand up quickly.

"What is it?"

"A dead rat. That explains the smell."

"Try again."

Will gave her a withering look and put his arm down once again. After feeling around, his hand brushed against something in the far corner. It had a rough texture and felt solid. When he tried to lift it, it was surprisingly heavy. He brought it up and set it down on the flagstones with a heavy metallic clunk. It was a bag made of rough sailcloth tied with a piece of string. The rats had nibbled a small hole in one corner, through which Will could see something that was a dull brownish colour. They looked at each other, hardly daring to open it, both knowing they were thinking the same thing. Will reached inside and brought out a long leather purse, bulging with something heavy. When he peered inside, a gasp escaped him.

Hannah had been watching impatiently and now she snatched the purse away from him. She pulled it open and tipped out the coins on to the floor. They tumbled out in a glistening heap, so many it was impossible to count them and each one as bright and alluring as sunlight. For a long time neither of them spoke. They both stared at the heap of golden guineas in baffled wonder. In the lamplight, the coins seemed to posses their own warmth – a fire that drew them in and robbed them of any desire to move or speak or leave that place. Will knew he wanted to keep this gold, to possess it, and he could see the same burning desire in Hannah's eyes. When she began to slip the guineas back into the leather purse, letting them trickle through her fist, he almost wanted to reach out and snatch it away from her.

"What are you doing?" he said.

"This way it will be easier to carry. Help me. We can hide the bag inside my basket."

"You mean *steal* it?"

Hannah stared at him as if he'd taken leave of his

senses. "Who are we stealing from? Him over there? He is dead, Will, dead as the grave. This gold is no good to him any more. Would you rather it stayed under the floor, gathering dust?"

He didn't know. He wanted to take it as much as Hannah, but it wasn't as simple as that. One man had already died for this gold.

"What if whoever did this comes looking for it?" He pointed to the body, lying beyond the table.

"They won't," said Hannah. "They'll never know." She returned to filling the leather purse. Will had to seize her by the wrist to make her look at him.

"Hannah! We know nothing about this money! How did it come here? Who were these men? If they were hiding gold in an empty house, then they must be robbers or highwaymen. This money is stolen."

"Even if it is, we can put it to honest use. You know why the doctor only visits my father once a week? Because my mother can't afford to pay his fees." She held out a handful of the shining guineas. "With this I can pay for a doctor to come every day, a whole tribe of doctors! Perhaps we'll even move away from Crowhurst and live in a grand house like my uncle."

Will could see the stubborn look in her eyes. Whatever he said, she would not listen. The gold had cast its spell and promised her everything she wanted. She gathered up the last of the guineas and dropped them into the leather purse, before replacing it in the bag and gently laying it in her basket. They were dragging the flagstone back into position when Will straightened up and listened.

"What is it?" asked Hannah.

"A horse, coming this way."

She heard it too. The beat of the hooves muffled by mud and leaves, but still audible, coming through the woods.

"Out the back!" whispered Will. "Not a sound."

Hannah snatched her basket from the table and they ran. The kitchen door was still ajar, and they burst through it into the yard. The house was built on the crest of a steep bank and they half ran, half slid down to the bottom. There they hid, lying on their stomachs among a thick clump of brown ferns, hardly daring to breathe.

Will felt Hannah's hand on his shoulder.

"The lantern!" she whispered urgently. "Did you bring the lantern?"

He stared at her. They had left it inside the house.

11

Hiding Place

For what seemed like an eternity they lay still, straining to hear what was happening in the cottage. Once Will thought he heard a horse snort in the dark, but then the wood was silent again. He could hear Hannah's shallow breathing beside him and see the shape of her dark head in profile. Whoever was inside the house was taking their time, and he wondered if even now they were searching the tub-hole under the stone floor. In their haste to escape, they had left the lantern in the middle of the floor where it was sure to be seen. It was too dark for them to see anything beyond the outline of the cottage roof above the bank. When they heard a door thud open, Will clung to the hope that the stranger was leaving. Instead, to his horror, he heard the man come out into the back yard. A few moments later he appeared at the top of the bank above them, bent over as if he was dragging a great weight. Will could hear the man grunting with the effort and heard him mutter an oath.

Then something came tumbling down from the top of the bank, rolling over and over until it came to a rest only a few feet from the spot where they were hiding. It was the corpse. Will could see the white face and the dark shadows that marked the sightless eyes. He heard a faint gasp escape from Hannah and prayed that she wouldn't give them away. The man at the top of the bank straightened up, and spat on the ground. He stood breathing heavily, looking down the hill into the woods beyond. He was only a black silhouette but they could see he was tall and powerfully built. Will pressed his cheek to the damp earth and didn't dare to move. Any moment now he felt sure the man would come down the bank and then he was sure to see them. Perhaps he would bury them in the woods along with the other body.

Instead the man retreated back to the house. Moments later they heard his horse carry him off through the trees. Will raised his head and let out a long breath.

"You saw him?" he said in a whisper.

"Not his face." He could see Hannah's shadow crouched beside him.

"You think he was the murderer?"

"No," said Hannah. "We heard him running away. Why would he come back?"

"Whoever he was, he was looking for the gold," said Will.

"Perhaps," said Hannah. "But he doesn't know we were here."

"What about the lantern? He would have seen it."

"Anyone could have left a lantern. Don't worry, Will. We're safe."

Safe? The word rung hollow. A few feet away from them the corpse lay sprawled at the bottom of the bank, with the white face turned to the sky. Will had the disturbing sensation that the eyes were staring up at him.

"Let's get away from this place," he said.

He waited outside while Hannah went back in the cottage to collect the lantern they'd left behind. A minute later, she returned empty-handed. It had gone. It struck Will as another bad sign. He would have gladly left the gold behind there and then, but Hannah stubbornly refused to consider it. There was nothing for it but to find their way back to the village in the dark.

Once out of the woods, they made for the coast road, knowing it would be easier to find their way along it in the dark. They made slow progress crossing the fields. Their wet clothes clung to them and they trudged on through the mud in silence. Hannah kept the sailcloth bag hidden at the bottom of her basket and Will noticed that every now and then she put her hand inside to make sure the precious cargo was still there. Several times he made them leave the road to hide among the trees, thinking that he heard someone following and imagining it was the horseman come to murder them.

When they finally came over the brow of the East Hill, they were both relieved to see the lights of the village below. But their good fortune didn't last. As they climbed Market Street, Lieutenant Lock was coming out of the Customs House and almost walked right into them.

"It's late to be out," he said shining his lantern in their faces so that they shrank from its harsh light. Hannah hid the basket behind her skirts and prayed fervently that he wouldn't notice it and ask to see what was inside.

"We were just on our way home, Lieutenant," she said.

"Miss Burrell, isn't it? You're staying at the Rectory?"

Hannah nodded.

"You shouldn't be wandering the streets after dark, Miss. Not with this escaped prisoner still on the loose."

"Then you haven't found him yet?" said Will. With all that had happened that night, he had almost forgotten his anxiety that Louis might have been captured.

"Not yet," said Lock, "but rest assured, we will have the villain soon. He can't have got far without money or friends, and my men are watching the roads. Oh yes, we'll have him, don't you worry about that." He paused, remembering they were little more than children and he was wasting his breath. "Well, your uncle will be waiting for you, Miss Burrell. Goodnight to you."

He touched his hat and strode off briskly down the hill.

Outside the Rectory, they paused in the lane. At the side of the house a light spilled from the study window, indicating that the Reverend Spencer was at home. Hannah knew she would face a severe inquisition for returning home so late. She hadn't seen her uncle since the previous morning when they'd left for Crowhurst.

Will pointed to the bag in the bottom of her basket. "I'll feel better when we've hidden this somewhere safe," he said.

"I've been thinking about that," said Hannah. "And I think we should keep it here."

"At the Rectory?" Will frowned. He had assumed they would hide the money at the Angel, though he hadn't yet decided on a safe place.

"Think, Will," Hannah said, "my uncle hardly ever

has visitors. There is only him and Mrs Lawson in the house."

"Mrs Lawson?"

"The housekeeper – but she only comes at ten and mostly keeps to the kitchen. Besides, who would look for a bag of gold in the house of a clergyman? It's the perfect place!"

"But where? Where would you hide it?" he asked.

"The one place my uncle never goes: in the garden. There's a tree by the south wall, a big old elm. Sometimes I climb up there when my uncle isn't at home. You can see over the whole village, right across to the sea. Halfway up the trunk there's a hole, big enough to push the bag inside where it'll be out of sight. That's where we'll hide it, Will. No one will ever know it's there!"

She beamed at him, pleased with her idea. Will wasn't sure. But it was true that few visitors ever came to the Rectory, and he had to admit he didn't have a better idea. It was as safe a place as any.

"All right," he said. "But promise me this, once it's hidden, you leave it alone."

"What do you mean?"

"I told you. We don't who the money belongs to. Perhaps it is stolen, perhaps someone's still looking for it. Until we find out, we shouldn't touch it."

Hannah folded her arms. "And how do you intend to find out?"

"We wait. Keep our ears open. A sack of gold guineas doesn't go missing every day. There must be hundreds in there. Someone in the village will have heard of something."

He could see Hannah didn't like the idea. She wanted to help her father now, while his need was desperate. But for once Will refused to be swayed by her arguments. The gold would stay hidden until they were satisfied there wasn't any danger. A few weeks, said Will, it wasn't long to wait.

For the next few days Will kept alert for news of a large sum of money that been lost or stolen. Yet no one in Lydwell appeared to have heard anything about it. Even the death of the man they'd found in the abandoned cottage seemed to have gone unreported. At the Angel, all the talk in the evenings was of the missing Frenchman, "the spy" who had escaped. Lieutenant Lock's volunteers had been searching all the outlying farms within five miles of Lydwell. Some were convinced that the spy's appearance had something to do with the invasion, and any day expected to see the French fleet off the coast of Sussex. A reward of one hundred pounds had been offered for information leading to the prisoner's arrest.

Will started to believe that Hannah had been right all along about the gold. It had belonged to the dead man and perhaps no one else knew of its existence. But early on a Thursday evening, four days after they had returned from Crowhurst, something happened to change his mind.

The stranger arrived at the Angel soon after seven o'clock. Will saw him cross the parlour and look into the snug, which at this hour of the evening was cold and empty. Returning to the parlour, he took a seat by the fire, holding out his hands to warm himself. He wore a broad-brimmed hat that shadowed his eyes, and a greatcoat, spattered with mud as if he'd ridden a long distance. When he leaned forward in his chair, rubbing his hands to bring the warmth back into them, the firelight caught his sullen features and Will knew that they'd met before. It was the man called Stubbs, one of Moses Morley's gang. Will wondered why he had strayed so far from home and what had brought him to the Angel Inn. He thought of the bag of gold guineas hidden in the hollow of the tree in the Rectory garden, and a sick feeling passed through him like a premonition. Had Stubbs's presence at the Angel something to do with the missing gold?

He busied himself behind the bar, trying to avoid the hunched figure by the fire. But Stubbs had taken off his hat and coat and was calling for rum, banging his fist on the table, drawing stares from the other occupants of the parlour, who looked away quickly when he scowled in their direction. When Will took him his drink, he gave no sign that he recognized him, but seized the boy's arm and hung on.

"There's a doctor lives hereabouts. Is he in tonight?"

"You mean Dr Rankin?" said Will.

"Rankin, aye, that's the fellow. Is he here? Point him out to me, boy. There's a matter I'd like to discuss with him, a private matter."

Will glanced down. The smuggler's hands were as black as coal. "The doctor doesn't usually come in till later," he told him.

"Then I'll wait," said Stubbs. "I'll wait." He pulled Will closer so he could feel his warm, sour-smelling breath. "But when he comes you'll be sure to point him out to me, boy, won't you? The minute he comes in." Will nodded and was finally released.

"Bring me another glass. . . No, wait boy, bring a bottle. There's money for you." He thrust his hand into his pocket and spilled a handful of coins on the table.

Stubbs waited for an hour, and then another hour, drinking rum steadily and staring moodily into the fire. Finally his temper and impatience got the better of him. He stood up, swaying slightly, and beckoned Will over.

"Where is he, your doctor friend? You told me he'd be here!"

"I don't know, sir. Perhaps he is not back from visiting one of his patients."

"Patients be damned! I've sat here these two hours and I'm sick to death of waiting. You give the good doctor a message from me. He's to be here tomorrow night at nine without fail. At nine. There's a friend of mine wants to meet him. Tell him we have business to discuss, a proposition."

"What name shall I give?" asked Will.

"Tell him Moses wants to see him. You won't forget a name like that, will you, boy?"

Will shook his head.

"Smart lad, smart lad." Stubbs shook the rum bottle to make sure it was empty. "Tomorrow night then. Be sure he gets the message to come at nine. My friend ain't a patient man and he don't like to be kept waiting."

Stubbs picked up the empty bottle and tossed it into the flames where it shattered, sending splinters of glass into the fireplace. The other customers in the parlour glanced up, but none of them dared to speak. They had seen the brace of pistols the smuggler had tucked in his belt. Stubbs glowered at them and made his way unsteadily to the door.

12

A Gathering of Wolves

The next evening Dr Rankin arrived by eight o'clock and took his usual seat in the snug, along with Liney Roach, Job Moss the blacksmith, and old Billy Hayes, whose brown face was framed by long white sideburns that swept down to the corners of his mouth. Hayes was a drayman who carried the beer barrels on his cart back and forth along the turnpike road from the brewery. As usual he was dressed in his square-cut, brown cloth coat with the leather patches on the elbows and shoulder. Will had never seen him remove this coat even in summer. Along with the other three, Hayes had been elected to meet Morley and represent the interests of the Lydwell smugglers, with Rankin as their principal spokesman. When Liney Roach sat back, Will noticed a knife peeping out from his belt, underneath his threadbare tailcoat. One seat was left vacant at the table, which was the place that Dutch would once have occupied. Since his death the smugglers' meetings had become more subdued affairs. Dutch had never been one to waste his words, but when he spoke the others listened, and his absence somehow made the room seem smaller.

Will brought them their drinks and lingered a while to listen to their talk. By now the smugglers were used to his presence and paid him little attention, accepting his right to stay if he wished.

"Never mind that, Billy," Roach was saying. "Why are we here? That's what I'd like to know. What does a blackhearted devil like Morley want with us?"

"That's what we're here to find out," said Dr Rankin. "They say Morley's gang has been seen as far west as Marden. The whole country is afraid of them. It's my belief he'll want to strike some kind of bargain."

"If he thinks we'll dance to his tune, he can think again," grumbled Roach.

"Well, let's hear him out," said Rankin. "I've no wish to make an enemy of Morley. Try to control that tongue of yours, Liney, and leave me to do the talking." He lit his clay pipe and watched the smoke curl from the bowl.

At just after nine, Will heard horses approaching along the lane. The others in the room heard it too and glanced at each other uneasily. Roach ran his finger back and forth along the flat of his knife until he caught the doctor's eye and slipped it away beneath his coat.

A few minutes later they heard heavy footsteps in the corridor and Moses Morley appeared in the doorway. He seemed to fill the tiny room on his own, and in the candlelight his pock-marked face with the broad flat nose was even uglier than Will remembered.

With him came four of his men, including his lieutenant, Stubbs. Will noticed that they were all armed with pistols at their belts. He shrank back in the shadows, hoping that Morley wouldn't recognize him from their last meeting in Crowhurst.

"You must be the doctor," said the gangleader, eyeing Rankin.

"And you must be the famous Moses Morley," said Dr Rankin rising to his feet. "Welcome to you, gentlemen. If you would be so good as to leave your weapons outside, then we can make ourselves comfortable and get down to business."

A dark shadow stole across Morley's face, but he controlled his temper. "Why not? We are all friends here, ain't we? Do as the doctor says, boys."

While the visitors divested themselves of their weapons, Will slipped out of the room to fetch their drinks. When he returned, the Crowhurst men had taken their seats, across the table from their hosts. Morley was in the middle, opposite the doctor, seated in the chair which was usually kept vacant for Dutch. Evidently no one had dared ask him to move. Will set down the bottle of rum and the glasses on the table. As he leaned over the table the candlelight fell on his face and a large hand reached out and clamped over his wrist. When he looked down he found Morley's cold black eyes staring into his.

"I seen you before, ain't I, boy?"

Will swallowed hard. His voice came out as dry as dust. "Yes sir. In Crowhurst."

"So it was, I remember you now. And here you are again. Strange how you keep turning up like a bad penny, ain't it?"

"Let him go," said Dr Rankin. "There is no mystery. The boy lives here at the inn with his mother. She is the landlady."

Morley didn't even glance at the doctor. He kept Will's hand imprisoned and his eyes never left him. "What's your name, boy?"

"Will Finch."

"Well, Mister Finch, bring a lantern, we are too much in the dark here, and I like to see who I'm talking to."

Will did as he was told, fetching the brass lantern from the window and placing it in the middle of the table. He wondered why Morley wanted it, since there was already a candle burning. But the smuggler hadn't finished with him yet.

"What say you, boy, are you afraid of me?" he asked.

Will gazed into the cruel face, scarred like old leather. "No sir."

"No? Then perhaps you don't know me well enough." Morley drew the lantern across the table towards him. He undid the catch, and pulled the glass door open so that the flame inside was bared. With the palm of his hand face down, he pushed it inside the lantern till it was suspended an inch above the flickering yellow flame. Lower and lower he brought his hand until everyone around the table could see the flame lick against his skin. A smell of burning flesh laced the air. For what seemed like a minute Morley kept his hand over the flame while nobody spoke or moved and the crazed smile never left his face. At last he drew his hand away and held up the palm to show them a dark spot the size of a penny where the candle had burned him.

"What about you, boy?" asked Morley, turning to Will. "You ain't afraid, are you? A brave lad like you. How much pain can you bear?" Morley took hold of Will's wrist and held it fast.

"No sir. Please!" said Will. He tried to resist, to pull his arm away, but the smuggler's strength was overpowering.

"This lantern here," said Morley. "It's not a common design. A cabin lantern, I'd say, wouldn't you, boy?"

Will didn't answer, his eyes fixed on the flame. He suddenly knew why Morley was playing this game and where it was leading.

"That's enough!" said Dr Rankin. "You're hurting the boy."

Morley paid no attention and forced Will's hand closer to the open back of the lamp.

"Suppose you had a pair of these but one of them went missing. Know anything about that?"

"No sir. That's the only lantern of that kind I've seen."

"The only one?" You wouldn't be lying to me now, Mister Finch?"

Will's hand was pushed inside the lantern, so close to the flame that he could feel its heat.

"The truth, boy."

"That's enough!" Dr Rankin thundered, pushing the lantern away. "I said let the boy go, Morley."

"As you wish, Doctor, as you wish," said Morley. "Here's money for the rum, boy. Take it."

He put his hand in his pocket and slipped a coin into Will's hand. Will stared at it. A golden guinea. He could feel his heart thumping against his ribs. What did Morley mean by it? Had he been there at the house in the woods that night? Did he know they had taken the gold? Will felt sure that the guilt was etched plain as day on his face. His hand was shaking and to hide it he slipped the coin in his pocket and stepped back from the table.

Morley turned his attention back to Rankin. "You know everything has its price, Doctor, even gold. One gold guinea can fetch up to thirty shillings."

"Indeed?" said the doctor.

"Oh, there are them that will pay that and more, believe me, if you know where to take it. Which is why I've put away a little gold myself, being a man of business. When there's a war on, gold is much in demand."

"You mean the Guinea Run?"

"Ah, then you've heard of it?"

"Forty-foot boats crossing the Channel from Deal with a crew manning the sweeps. They say they can carry as much as thirty thousand guineas in one trip."

"You're a clever fellow, Doctor, work it out then. Thirty shillings for every one of those shiners, that's a handsome profit, wouldn't you say?"

"You may be right, but what has this to do with us? We're not in the market for smuggling gold."

"Just this," Morley leaned over the table and narrowed his eyes. "Some rogue has been stealing from me. The gold was stowed in a dozen different places for safe keeping. But last Sunday two hundred guineas was took from a place in Blackthorn Woods.

You wouldn't have heard any tales about that, I suppose?"

"Nothing at all," replied Dr Rankin coolly. "Perhaps it was one of your own men."

"Oh, they know me better than that," said Morley. "If they so much as touched a penny of mine I would hang them from the nearest tree and leave the ravens to peck out their eyes. No, the villain that did this came from around here. The woods are close and there's this matter of the lantern too. Show him, Stubbs."

Stubbs set a lantern down on the table. It was made of brass and matched the other lantern on the table in every particular. A ship's cabin lantern, heavy and solid with a ring to hang it from the ceiling. Beyond any shadow of a doubt Will knew it was the same lantern they had left behind in the house in the woods.

"Someone left this in the house where the gold was hidden," said Morley.

"What of it? There may be a hundred lanterns that look like that," replied the doctor.

"Not so many, I've been looking. But strange I should find one here that's as like as two farthings. Perhaps the thief is sitting in this very room now." His black eyes scanned their faces and Will shrank back against the wall, avoiding his gaze. "Be sure of this, Doctor," said Morley, "whoever took the gold, I will find them out."

"Is that why you're here? You came all this way because you think we stole your damned two hundred guineas?" asked Rankin.

Morley laughed harshly and sat back in his chair. "You're right. We have more important business to talk about, you and me. Let's have another round of rum."

For a while the talk turned to smuggling and the hazards of bringing cargoes from France with the navy watching the coast. But Will was hardly listening. All he could think of was the bag of gold guineas hidden in the hollow of the tree in the Rectory garden. It had been smugglers' gold all along. Will had never heard of the Guinea Run, but he supposed that gold guineas could be smuggled in the same way as spirits and tobacco. Yet Dr Rankin had implied the guineas didn't come into the country, they were smuggled out, where they could be sold abroad at a higher price. Who bought them, Will had no idea; what mattered was that the gold belonged to Moses Morley. Morley had the lamp and now he suspected it had come from the Angel. How long before he discovered who had taken the gold?

"Well then, let's come to the point," Dr Rankin was saying. "You said there was a matter you wished to put to us?"

Morley drained the last drops of rum from the bottom of his glass and set it down on the table. "I can see you're a man of business like me, Doctor, and I respect that, so I won't waste your time. Here is the long and short of it. You may have heard I carry on a pretty tidy trade in Kent."

"I'm sure of it," said the doctor.

"The Preventive don't come near the marshes. Too scared," said Morley. "They've heard what I do to Revenue men. But with you, things are different. Day and night they're watching you, trying to catch you in their net."

"We haven't been caught yet," said Rankin.

"But one day you will be, mark my words. Unless you strike first. And that's where I can help you, Doctor. I can arrange things so they'll leave you in peace."

The doctor drew on his pipe. "And how would you do that? There are five men stationed here at the Customs House. They all go armed with swords and pistols."

"Whereas your men carry nothing but bats," said Morley.

"Naturally."

"Then what if you was armed too, Doctor, to even things up a little? What if you carried muskets and pistols like my men? That would change things, wouldn't it? With fifty men you would have an army!"

"We've never carried guns," said Rankin. "I've no wish to start a war."

"Times are changing," replied Morley.

The doctor glanced at Liney Roach, who was sitting stiffly beside him, keeping himself in check with an effort.

"Say we entered into such a bargain," said Rankin, "I'm curious, what would you get in return?"

"Nothing but my fair share," replied Morley. "We split the profits down the middle, half to me, half to you and rich pickings for all of us. What do you say, Doctor? You won't get a fairer offer."

The room had grown quiet and Will felt the weight of the silence. Apart from Rankin, the Lydwell men had listened without a word. Job Moss was looking ill at ease, while old Billy Hayes pulled at his side-whiskers and stared at the table glumly. Only Liney Roach fixed his bloodshot eyes on Morley with a look of ill-concealed contempt. They all knew that Morley's offer was little short of blackmail. Either they cooperated and meekly yielded the half share he wanted, or else he would compel them by force. He had made it clear to them that his men were well armed. Other smuggling gangs in Kent had already been threatened and forced to join Morley's growing empire.

Dr Rankin took out his pipe and glanced at the men sitting beside him. "You want our answer?" he said. "Very well then, here it is. We want nothing from you, Morley, not your advice nor your damned weapons. And we'll not be paying you a half share either. Our answer is no. Not in a thousand years."

Morley kept very still. Only his black eyes moved. "Think again, Doctor. I made you a handsome offer. Take it while you have the chance."

"Is that a threat?" said Rankin.

"A friendly warning," said Morley. "I get what I want sooner or later. Ask anyone."

Liney Roach spoke at last, pushing his wrinkled face forward. "You heard what the doctor said. Crawl back to the dunghill where you came from, you pox-ridden villain."

Morley turned his head slowly towards the undertaker, his eyes glittering with hatred. Suddenly his right hand slipped inside his coat. But before he could pull out the pistol he had concealed, Roach had the point of his knife at Morley's throat.

"No tricks, my bonny lad," he said. "Now you and your friends saddle your horses and be on your way. It's a long ride back to the marshes."

Morley rose to his feet, his face white with anger. He took one last look at them, as if committing each of their faces to memory, and swept out of the room. Will waited until he heard their horses clatter past the front of the inn and down the narrow lane, then he sunk down into his seat beside Job Moss.

Dr Rankin looked at him curiously and poured a glass of rum. "Here," he said. "You'd better take this, Will. You look as if you've seen a ghost."

13

Divided

That night Will's dreams were full of Moses Morley. He found himself back in the wood, running wildly, stumbling and crashing through the undergrowth. He knew he had to escape from the horseman who was following him and was there whenever he looked back. The top of a steep bank rose into view and he slid down it, losing his footing, sliding and tumbling down in his blind panic. There was the ruined cottage, just as he remembered it. Inside, a fire was burning in the grate, the flames casting dancing shadows on the floor. Small pieces of dust and twigs fell from the roof like snow, landing on his hair and shoulders as he moved around like a sleepwalker. Then he was down on his hands and knees, searching for the loose flagstone in the floor, knowing there wasn't much time. His fingers found the edge and he peered down into the yawning black hole beneath, hoping to see a gleam of gold. Instead a shape swam into view, pale and white, floating below him. Moses Morley's face rose up out of the dark, with a neat red hole in the middle of his forehead where the bullet had entered. His dead man's eyes snapped open and his withered hand reached up to fasten round Will's neck, pulling him down into the foul-smelling darkness and the earth.

Will let out a shrill cry of terror and awoke to find himself sitting up in bed in his room at the Angel, with his mother knocking on the door.

That morning at school he waited impatiently for a chance to speak to Hannah. When they were allowed out into the yard at midday, he found his way to the porch at the back of the schoolhouse. Here there was a back door which Miss Parkes always kept locked. Three steps led up to a brick porch with a gabled roof. It was out of the sight of the rest of the schoolyard and a place where few of the children came.

Hannah arrived a few minutes later, as they had arranged. "What's the matter?" she asked, seeing his worried face. It didn't take him long to explain. He told her about Morley's visit the previous night and the conversation he had overheard. He even confessed that the villagers who had come to the meeting were smugglers and that some of them were his friends (though he took care not to mention any names). Finally, he drew the golden guinea from his pocket and repeated the threats that Morley had made. Hannah listened in silence, visibly shaken. In her mind, Morley belonged to the nightmare world of the marshes and it was hard to believe that he had followed them here to Lydwell. Yet, despite everything, she remained stubbornly determined to keep the gold.

"We're still safe," she argued. "He doesn't know who took the money."

"He has the lantern," said Will. "Sooner or later he'll find out it belonged to us."

"How will he? He can't be sure it came from the inn. And even if it did, anyone could have taken it and left it in that house. Morley won't be looking for two children."

Will shook his head. "He was there that night, he must have been. Remember the man we saw drag the body from the house and push it down the bank? It was Morley, I'm sure of it. He must have found the lantern and kept it."

"What does it matter?" replied Hannah. "He didn't see us. In any case, what was he doing there? Why did they keep the gold somewhere so far from Crowhurst?"

"I don't know," admitted Will. "All I know is we

can't keep the money now. As long we have it we're in terrible danger. He'll kill us if he finds out, Hannah."

"He won't, it's safe where it is," she said confidently. "All we need to do is sit tight and keep our heads."

From the schoolyard round the corner came the sound of children's voices chanting a playground rhyme. Will almost envied them their innocence. He took a deep breath. He hadn't yet told her what he'd decided that morning. The worst part of all.

"Listen to me, Hannah. We have to take the money back. All of it."

"Back?" she stared at him as if he'd taken leave of his senses. "Go back to that house?"

"I've been over it a thousand times and there's no other way. As long as the money is missing, Morley will go on searching for it and we'll never be safe. We have to take it back."

Hannah folded her arms and leaned back against the porch. When she raised her head he saw the old look of defiance.

"No," she said flatly. "Not now, not after all we went through."

"Hannah!"

"You do what you like, but half of it is rightfully mine."

He was about to argue, to try and make her see reason, but from round the corner of the schoolhouse he heard a distinct sound, a whisper followed by suppressed laughter. Will put a finger to his lips and stepped down from the porch. He reached the corner of the wall and almost walked straight into Robert Newson who was crouched behind it, with Jack Merrit behind him. They ran away, shrieking with idiotic laughter.

"Hannah!" they called to each other. "Hannah, my love, my angel!"

Will felt his face flush scarlet. When he turned back to the porch, he could see Hannah had heard them too. She shrugged her shoulders, dismissing them scornfully.

"Do you think they heard?" he asked.

"That pair of dunces? They think we're sweethearts, that's all."

He avoided looking at her, feeling suddenly awkward. But he wasn't sure if she was right. He wondered how long Newson had been crouching behind the wall, and how much he had heard. He certainly would have pricked up his ears if he had heard them mention gold. Will thought back over their conversation, trying to remember if either of them had let slip where the money was hidden. He didn't think so, but he couldn't be certain. They would have to return the gold soon, he decided, perhaps even that night. But first he would have to persuade Hannah.

* * *

On the way home from school they were both preoccupied with their own thoughts. Once the gold had drawn them together – a secret shared only by the two of them – now Will felt it was driving a wedge between them. He blamed Hannah – she was the one who had insisted they take the money – but in his heart he knew that he'd wanted it just as badly. The truth was, the gold had cast a spell over both of them from the moment they'd set eyes on it. Will remembered the weight of the bag when he'd brought it up out of the hole and the way the glittering coins had spilled on to the floor and taken his breath away. "Shiners" Morley had called them. Part of him understood why Hannah couldn't bring herself to give the gold up, why she was even willing to risk their lives in order to keep it. She believed that Morley's gold was her passport to a better life; it would cure her father's fever and bring her family back together. It had come to her like a miracle and she put her faith in it because she had nothing else to believe in.

They had reached the Rectory, both of them so absorbed that they had hardly spoken a word for most of the way.

"Let's not argue," said Will, as if she could read his thoughts.

Hannah turned to face him. "Then you agree? We'll keep it?"

"For tonight," he said, evasively. "But Hannah, let's move it to a safer place. I'm worried that Newson might have heard us talking!"

She agreed readily, glad that he was no longer insisting on going back to the house in the woods. They both knew they were merely postponing a decision. They would take the sailcloth bag and bury it in a remote spot. Will knew a place on the West Hill, close to the castle ruins.

Hannah led him out into the garden. It was late afternoon and at this time her uncle was seldom at home, whilst Mrs Lawson, the sour-faced house-keeper, would be busy in the kitchen preparing that evening's supper. No one was likely to disturb them. The old elm tree stood in the far corner of the garden by the south wall. With its arching, sinewy branches, it was the kind of tree that almost begged to be climbed. Hannah pointed upwards to a fork in the trunk high above their heads, where Will could see a dark oval hole, as big as a fist.

"You stay here," he said. "I'll climb up and throw it down to you."

She slanted her eyes at him. "You think you'd reach it before me?"

In a moment they had both reached up for the lowest branch and were climbing in an eager race to reach the hiding place first. In his jacket and breeches, Will was better dressed for climbing, but even encumbered by her long dress, Hannah kept pace with him. He was climbing the tree for the first time, whereas she had already discovered the best branches and footholds. They clambered up, as agile as two monkeys, both absorbed wholly in the pleasure of scaling the tree. Finally Will got one hand on the branch and hoisted himself up to sit astride it, just as Hannah came round the other side of the trunk, having taken another route.

"I beat you," he said, out of breath.

"You lying dog!" She laughed. "It was a draw!"

They sat astride the branch side by side, looking out from their perch high above the garden. The afternoon sun was low in the sky, bathing the hills in warm golden light. From here the village was a patchwork of red-tiled roofs and chimneys, with the tall tower of St Michael's Church like a sentinel above the sea. Will felt he would have gladly stayed there for a long time. All his problems – the threat posed by Morley and his anxiety for Louis's safety – belonged in the village far below; up here nothing could reach him. Hannah must have felt something similar, because for a long time the two of them sat watching the sun make its slow descent beneath the West Hill. Eventually it was Hannah who broke the spell. She shifted her position closer to the trunk of the tree and leaned over until she could thrust her hand into the bole hole. She felt around, pushing her arm in further, up to the elbow. Will watched her expression turn from puzzlement to a look of dismay.

"It's not there," she said, withdrawing her hand.

He laughed, not believing her. "Don't play games, Hannah. Give it to me."

"I mean it. The bag's gone, Will. Someone must have taken it."

14

Cruel Warning

Will had plenty to occupy his thoughts as he set off the next morning for the lime kilns. The two hundred guineas had vanished without a trace, and neither he nor Hannah could be sure who had taken it. Initially Hannah was ready to accuse Robert Newson. Newson was certainly capable of stealing and he had been eavesdropping on them the previous day in the school-yard with Jack Merrit. But Will was fairly certain that neither of them had mentioned the exact location of the hiding place. In any case, he pointed out, when did Newson have the opportunity to steal the money? After school they had walked straight back to the Rectory and there would scarcely have been time for Newson to reach the Rectory garden, climb the tree and escape before they arrived.

Yet if Newson wasn't the culprit, then someone else must have known about the whereabouts of the gold. Hannah swore that neither her uncle or his housekeeper could have known anything about it. That left the possibility that Morley or someone else had taken the money, yet neither Will nor Hannah had mentioned the secret to anyone. They decided to keep a close eye on Robert Newson and Jack Merrit at school, hoping that sooner or later the thief would betray themselves by some word or action.

Hannah had reacted to the theft of the money with a mixture of fury and despair. In contrast, Will found that he was actually relieved. He had woken up that morning feeling that a weight had been lifted from his shoulders. Morley's gold had gone and he, for one, hoped they would never see it again. No one knew that he and Hannah had stolen the money in the first place, and now it had disappeared, there was nothing to link them to it. Perhaps they were free. If he was honest, Will had dreaded the prospect of returning to the abandoned house in the wood, but now there was no need.

As he climbed out of the village and crested the East Hill, the sky was the palest of blues and the trees and fields were bathed in watery sunshine. Will felt almost light-hearted. He had seen little of Louis since his return from Crowhurst. Now the only thing that concerned him was helping the Frenchman to escape the country. The soldiers had abandoned their search for the missing prisoner, sharing in the general belief that he was either dead or must have found a boat to take him back to France. Only Lieutenant Lock persisted in setting a watch on the roads around Lydwell.

Will was looking forward to seeing Louis again. Today he had brought him a bottle of brandy to make up for his neglect of the past few days. In less than an hour he was nearing the lime kilns and came to the place where the path began to descend towards the sea in a series of twists and turns. To his left he could see the turnpike road winding through the trees, the route he had travelled to Crowhurst perched on top of the stagecoach. It was only the previous Saturday but already it seemed like a lifetime ago.

When he heard a vehicle approaching on the road ahead, he instinctively drew back out of sight. The volunteers were sometimes out marching the roads early in the morning and he had no wish to run into Lieutenant Lock. He was greatly relieved when a cart drew into sight around the bend, pulled by a heavy shire horse that plodded along the road at a snail's pace. As it drew closer Will recognized the ancient dray cart which old Billy Hayes drove back and forth along the road, ferrying barrels of ale from Carsley's Brewery. He expected to see Hayes in the driver's seat in his patched, brown cloth coat, looking like he'd been carved out of walnut. But today the driver's seat was empty and the horse appeared to be making her way home all by herself.

Will wondered if Hayes had stopped at an inn and had laced his breakfast with too much rum, with the result that he'd fallen into a ditch on the wayside. But Hayes was a stolid, reliable character, regular in his habits and mindful of his duties. It would be unlike him to get drunk at this hour of the day. Will began to feel that something was wrong. The cart was now almost level with him and had come to a halt across the road, while the black horse paused to chew on some long grass. Abandoning the path, Will went towards it.

The horse raised her head when he drew near, as if she was pleased to see another living creature. She seemed restless and skittish, tossing her head up and down. Will patted her neck and soothed her, speaking reassuringly. He could see the reins lying idly across the driver's seat along with Billy Hayes's long whip. The cart was stacked with tall oak casks in rows of three, packed close together. Nothing looked out of place, yet somehow the eerie quiet of the road and the empty driver's seat disturbed him. When he approached the back of the cart, he did so warily, almost as if he sensed what he would find.

Billy Hayes was in the back of the cart, propped between two barrels. His back was against the high wooden side and his head lolled forward on his chest, as if he had fallen into a deep sleep. His legs were thrust out in front of him with his scuffed black leather boots resting against one of the barrels that he had carried so often on his back.

"Mister Hayes?" said Will, but he knew he was wasting his breath, and spoke only for the reassurance of hearing his own voice. When he climbed up into the cart and knelt beside the body, he could see the pallor of the old man's face, his bruised and swollen cheeks, with the mouth gaping open as if he was trying to cry out. There was something white behind his teeth. His patched brown cloth coat had been stripped from his back, and a dark stain spread across his belly. The blood had formed in a pool on the floor, as dark and thick as molasses. Will stood up quickly and clasped a hand over his mouth, feeling his gorge rising. He climbed down and stood at the side of the road, taking deep draughts of air to quell the sickness in his stomach. A moment later he broke into a run, not knowing where he was going, wanting only to escape from the cart and the body propped up in the back.

In a few minutes he came to a halt, finding himself at the lime kilns. Louis was close by, he remembered – that was the reason he had set out from the village early that morning.

It didn't take him long to reach the mouth of the cave and to squeeze his body through the narrow passageway. Inside, he was surprised to hear voices at the back of the cave, voices that died away abruptly when his footsteps approached. In the cave's main chamber, he found a low fire burning and Louis standing in its smoke, pointing a pistol straight at him. Will was so taken aback that he didn't hear the movement behind him before it was too late. A strong arm gripped him round the throat, choking the breath out of him.

"And who are you, mate?" said the man who held him prisoner. "Speak up. How did you find us?"

Louis lowered the pistol and laughed. "Let him go, Joseph! He's a friend. This is the boy I told you about."

Will felt the arm holding him relax and turned to see a lean, hungry-looking man, dressed in the short blue jacket of the King's Navy. His coarse grey hair was tied back in a pig-tail with a black ribbon and when he spoke he nodded repeatedly to give his words extra emphasis.

"Beggin' your pardon, lad, I didn't mean to hurt you. I thought you was maybe one of them redcoats that's out looking for my friend here. Next time, you sing out clear as a bell so we know you're coming. Sing out your name and we'll know who it is."

Will promised that he would remember next time. In his eagerness to find Louis he had completely forgotten that he should have given a signal before entering the cave.

Louis was hastily putting away some papers the two men had evidently been studying when he walked in on them. Will caught a glimpse of a small grey book before it was spirited away into a wooden chest along with the papers.

"Come, sit by the fire and warm yourself, Will," said Louis. "You look cold. We were just looking at some letters that Joseph brought me from Brighton. He has kindly been helping me with this business of my grandfather's will."

Joseph nodded at him and gave a conspiratorial wink. "Matters of law, Will, matters of law. Not that they mean much to a simple cove like me what can scarce read or write. I'm just the messenger I am, I does what I'm told."

"So, where have you been?" asked Louis. "I was beginning to think you had quite abandoned me."

Will finally had the chance to tell them what he had seen on the road and describe the poor bloodied corpse in the back of the dray cart. The two men listened to him, exchanging glances with each other. "I can show you the place where I left him," Will told them. "If we go now the cart may still be there."

The bluejacket, Joseph, rubbed his chin. "I don't know. Maybe we should leave well alone. It sounds a bad business all right, and from what you say, this ain't the work of robbers or they would have taken the liquor. They gave this fellow a bad beating. And why send him home like that, trussed up in the back of the cart?"

"Perhaps to teach someone a lesson," said Louis, thoughtfully.

"You may be right," said Joseph, nodding and rising to his feet. "But if you'll take my advice, you'll leave it to the law. Someone will find the body soon enough, let 'em make it their business. What's it to do with you and me?"

"I knew Mister Hayes," said Will. "I can't just leave him there. It doesn't seem right."

Louis nodded. "Don't worry. I'll come back with you, Will. We'll take a look together."

Will gave him a grateful smile. He didn't know if he had the courage to return to the cart on his own and face what was in the back. Louis was taking a grave risk in accompanying him to the road in broad daylight, but he had no one else to ask. He waited a little way off, as Louis took leave of his visitor by the mouth of the cave. The two men talked in low voices and finally shook hands, before the seaman climbed the path and the blue of his jacket disappeared into the trees.

Will was puzzled by the sudden appearance of this man. Where had he sprung from and how had he known where to find Louis? His role in the matter surrounding the house and estate in Brighton seemed equally obscure. Who did Louis know who would be sending him papers to read? Will decided to try and find out more as soon as he had the chance. For now there was the more pressing matter of Billy Hayes's body.

When they reached the bend in the turnpike road there was no sign of the dray cart. They eventually found it a little further down the highway, where the cart had trailed off the lane, coming to rest under some horse chestnut trees. The black horse was grazing contentedly in the long grass, evidently in no hurry to make its way home. When they approached the cart, Will could see the old drayman's body still propped up in the back.

"You wait there and keep watch on the road," Louis told him. "If you hear anyone coming, be sure to let me know."

Will nodded, relieved that he didn't have to look at Billy Hayes's poor battered face again. He stood behind the cart, facing along the turnpike road towards the village, while Louis climbed into the back and squeezed himself between the rows of barrels. He was gone only a minute, but when he returned he had something in his hand. Will saw it was a piece of paper, rolled tight into a ball.

"What is it?" he asked.

"I have seen dead men before, but this. . ." Louis shook his head in disgust. "They tied him up and beat him like a dog, then stuffed this ball of paper inside his mouth. If he wasn't dead already it would have choked him."

Will remembered that he had glimpsed something white inside Hayes's gaping mouth. Louis unfolded the piece of paper, which was scrawled with a crudely written message:

Look on the death that will be yours. Them who will not join me I count my enemys. I know you for the damned villayns you are. Return what you stowl or do not think to find mersy at my hands. You have until noon on Friday.

Louis gave Will the message to read for himself.

"Does this mean anything to you?"

"Morley," said Will. "It's from a man named Moses Morley. No one else could have done this."

Louis looked at the piece of paper thoughtfully. "I've heard the name before. A smuggler, I believe, like your friends in the village."

Will looked at him in surprise. "How long have you known that?"

"I'm not blind or a fool. Why else is there a tunnel under the Angel that comes out close to the cliffs? And barrels by the score hidden in a storeroom under a graveyard? If you want my help, Will, you'll have to speak plainly and tell me the truth. What does this fellow Morley want with you?"

Will saw there was no point in keeping secrets any longer. He told Louis everything he knew about Moses

Morley, beginning with the first time he had encountered him. He described Morley's visit to the Angel on Friday evening and the proposition he had put to the Lydwell smugglers.

"But your friends wouldn't agree?"

"They would never join with a man like Morley," said Will. "They'd rather die."

"He claims you stole something from him."

"Gold," said Will. "Two hundred gold guineas."

Louis pushed his fair hair back from his forehead. "Two hundred guineas? That's a pretty sum, Will. Do you have the money?"

"No," said Will. "That's the trouble. We found the money in a cottage in the woods near here. It was hidden under the floor."

"We? Who else was there?"

"Hannah, the girl I told you about. We were looking for you but you'd gone from the cave."

"Go on."

"We found a man in the house, a dead man. I don't know who he was."

"But you think this Moses fellow killed him?"

"Perhaps, I'm not sure. Someone else had been there and I think they were searching for the gold. But they didn't find where it was hidden."

"Then where's the money now?"

"It's disappeared. I swear on my life, I don't know where it is."

Will felt the hopelessness of the situation as he tried to explain. Billy Hayes was dead and before Morley had finished, perhaps more of his friends would die. The message scrawled on the piece of paper was a clear warning – either they accepted the "offer" put to them at the Angel or they would pay with their lives. The stolen guineas had only served to inflame Morley against them further. Perhaps poor Billy Hayes had confessed that his friends had taken the gold in the hope it would save his life.

Louis drew him behind the trees, out of sight of the road. "It's dangerous for me to be seen here," he said. "Can you drive the cart back to the village, with the body in the back?"

Will nodded. He'd ridden in the cart with Billy Hayes and knew that the horse was docile and could find its way home. If he kept his eyes fixed on the road ahead and didn't let them stray to what was in the back of the cart, he thought he could manage it.

Louis gave him the piece of paper with Morley's message. "Take this and show it to your friends," he said. "Tell them to come to the Angel tomorrow night."

"What are you going to do?" asked Will.

"You helped me once, when my life was in danger," said Louis. "Perhaps it's time I repaid the debt."

15

Council of War

The following night the smugglers were called to a meeting at the Angel Inn. News of the murder of Billy Hayes had spread fast and little else had been talked about in the village, since Will had arrived home with the body in the back of the cart.

After eight o'clock Will saw the first of the smugglers slip in to the parlour, where they stood by the fire warming themselves and sipping their rum. Others followed soon after: farmers and labourers coming in from the country along with coopers, fishermen, shop-keepers and sail-makers – all of them relying on the free trade to supplement their meagre incomes. They crowded into the smoky, low-ceilinged parlour until every seat was filled and the air was heavy with the smell of beer and tobacco. Will was kept busy ferrying drinks back and forth from the bar, but he noticed that tonight the usual laughter and merriment was absent from the parlour. Men talked together in low voices, shaking their heads and pulling at their beards. Everywhere Will heard the name of Morley, and often the speaker looked about him, as if he thought there might be danger in speaking that detested name out loud.

When they were all assembled and a lookout posted at the door, Dr Rankin rose to his feet. He stood with his back to the fire, drawing on his long-stemmed clay pipe and waiting for the murmur of voices to subside. From his place, Will had a good view of the doctor's sombre, determined face.

"Two nights ago," said Rankin, "I sat in the back room there with Billy Hayes on my left. Now Billy's dead, God rest his soul, and you know well as I who murdered him."

There was a rumble of discontent from the men in front of him. One or two at the back craned their necks to get a view of the doctor's face.

"I called you here tonight because we must give an answer and it must be the will of us all. You know what Morley wants. . ."

"Aye, to bleed us dry!" called out someone.

"In plain language, are we to be our own masters or are we to serve Moses Morley?" said Dr Rankin. "He offers us his protection, says he'll arm us against the

Revenue. But the offer comes at a price: half he profits from every cargo we bring home."

There were angry jeers in response to this. Dr Rankin held up his hand for silence.

"We must make our choice. Do we join Morley? Or are you prepared to fight him?"

The men began to shout all at once. "Join with Morley?" said Liney Roach. "I'd rather make a pact with the devil. Hang him, say I."

But other voices disagreed. They did not have the strength to fight Morley, they said.

A farmer named Ballard stepped forward into the light of the fire. He was red-faced and as stocky as a bullock, with a growling, belligerent voice that could be heard at the back of the room.

"You all heard what happened to poor Billy. Well, I was there when they lifted him down from the back of his cart. I saw what Morley did to him and I tell you this: he will do the same to each one of you." The talk had died down and Will saw that Ballard had got the attention of his audience. "Some of you talk of fighting. That's all well and good, but I have a wife and five children at home. How do I protect them if Morley and his gang come here? For come they will, tomorrow noon. How long do you think we'll hold out when they have guns and horses?"

The men stared back at him in silence. They had no answers. Many of them had families of their own and they'd all heard the rumours of what had happened in other villages over the Kent border. Morley's name struck fear into their hearts.

The silence was broken by the mocking voice of Liney Roach. "Oh, you was always a brave one, Tom Ballard."

The farmer picked out the wrinkled face of the undertaker in the middle of the crowd and threw back an insult. In a few moments the orderly meeting threatened to become a brawl, with men jabbing their fingers angrily and accusing one another of cowardice or worse. Ballard was trying to push his way through the crowd to reach Liney Roach and it was hard to tell whether men were trying to hold him back or urge him on. Dr Rankin's cries for order went unheard. None of them noticed the man in the brown tailcoat push his way to the front and raise the pistol in the air above his head. The sound of the gunshot was like a cannon going off in the crowded room and everyone turned to see who had fired.

Louis stood before them, the pistol still raised above his head, one side of his face in shadow, the other lit by the red glow of the fire. He was dirty, unshaven and wearing borrowed, ill-fitting clothes. Nevertheless he commanded their attention as one who was well used to addressing a crowd. "Thank you, gentlemen. Now, since you've all had your say, perhaps you would have the goodness to listen to me."

"And who the devil are you?" demanded a voice.

"My name is Louis Moreau."

"By God, it's the Frenchman!" A murmur of astonishment went round the room.

The farmer, Ballard, spoke out of the crowd and elbowed his way forward again. "Well, well. You've got a nerve walking in here, bold as brass. They've been searching for you all over."

"Let him alone, Tom," said Dr Rankin. "He's taken a risk in coming here tonight. Let's hear what he has to say."

Ballard spat on the floor. "He can save his breath, Doctor. We don't need any lessons from his kind."

"No, indeed," replied Louis. "When it comes to running away I have nothing to teach you."

"How's that?" said Ballard, eyeing him dangerously. "Are you calling me a coward, you damned Frog? I'll cut out your lying tongue!"

Ballard pulled something from his belt and Will saw the blade of a knife flash silver in the firelight.

"I did not come here to fight," said Louis.

"Don't you worry," gloated Ballard. "This ain't going to be a fight."

Will watched helplessly. He had hoped Louis would come, but he hadn't given any thought to the reception he would receive at the hands of the smugglers. Now he saw it had been a mistake. Ballard was closing in and Louis backed away towards the fireplace. No one in the room moved to help him. They were waiting to see what would happen. Louis was almost on top of the grate but with one quick movement he bent towards the fire, and when he whirled around the iron poker was grasped in his right hand. He pointed it at his opponent as if this was a fencing match and the poker his foil. The confidence drained a little from Ballard's face, but he crouched in readiness, knowing that if he could get under the Frenchman's guard, the knife would do its work.

For a moment the two men stood a few paces apart, their shapes silhouetted against the bright flames, the tall, fair-haired Frenchman in marked contrast to the stocky, scowling farmer. Suddenly Ballard made a rush, charging head down like a bull, seeking to catch his opponent unaware and thrust home the knife. Will saw the poker in Louis's hand cut the air and the next moment the knife had spun to the floor and Ballard was holding his wrist in pain. The next blow took the farmer in the soft of his belly and had him doubled over gasping for breath, before the third cracked down like a whip on his back, forcing him to sink to his knees. The fight had lasted no more than a few seconds. Louis pushed the tip of the poker into the folds of Ballard's fat neck.

"You are lucky, my friend," he said quietly. "If this was a sword, you would be dead. Now perhaps you'll do me the favour of letting me speak."

After that Louis suffered no more interruptions. Ballard was helped away through the crowd by some of his friends. Louis had their full attention now and he didn't waste it.

"Gentlemen," he said. "I'm told you are smugglers. You know the coast and the tides, you know the place to land a cargo, what it will fetch and what profit you will make. I know nothing of these things, but I know a little about soldiering. For five years I was an officer in the army and had the honour to serve under General Pichegru in the Rhine. I have fought many battles and one thing I can tell you is how to defend a town or a village against an attack."

"Are you offering to help us fight Morley?" asked Dr Rankin.

"If you want my help."

"But why?" asked the doctor, mystified. "What have you to gain?"

"Let us say I'm repaying a debt," replied Louis. "If it wasn't for your friend, Dutch, I would have perished that night the ship struck the reef. I never had a chance to thank him."

"This is no business of yours. Why should we trust you?" The voice belonged to Liney Roach.

"Do you have any choice?" asked Louis. "Are there any soldiers among you? Any that know how to form ranks and face a cavalry charge?"

No one spoke.

"Or perhaps you'd rather go crawling to this fellow Morley?"

"Never! I'd rather dig my own grave," said Roach.

"Then we don't have much time," said Louis. "Tomorrow is Friday and they will be here by noon. Choose now. Are you going to run – or fight like men?"

Voices answered, a few at first, then swelling to a tide, a roar of defiance that came from every corner of the room. The smugglers stamped their feet and hammered on the tables with their fists. Louis had succeeded in uniting them and giving them renewed hope. As Will added his voice to the rest, he hoped that the Frenchman could deliver what he promised.

16

Resistance

Once the meeting was over the men dispersed with instructions to meet back at the Angel early the next morning. Dr Rankin stood at the door to say goodnight to each of them, shaking them by the hand and speaking to each by name. Only the farmer, Ballard, pushed past without a word, glaring malevolently back at Louis. Will heard him grumbling loudly to his friends as they went off down the street and wondered how many of them would be back in the morning. Some of the younger ones had joined the Volunteers and had been drilled in firing practice at the Priory Meadows under the stern eye of Lieutenant Lock; but that was shooting at targets, tomorrow they would have to face an enemy that was flesh and blood.

When they had all gone, Dr Rankin returned to the table closest to the fire, where Louis and Liney Roach were already seated. By now it was past midnight, but Will had never felt so awake in his life. Tomorrow a battle would be fought in the streets of his own village, and he would play his part in it. When the time came he wondered if he would prove himself or whether his courage would desert him. He was so lost in his own thoughts that he was surprised when his mother set down a bottle of port wine on the table and took her place beside him to listen. All evening she had been kept busy and Will remembered guiltily that once Dr Rankin had begun to speak he'd forgotten all about his serving duties.

Louis was studying a creased and dog-eared map that the doctor had unfolded on the table. It showed Lydwell and the countryside around, divided into a patchwork of fields, with the woods and forests picked out like grey islands. The village was divided by the two main roads of Market Street and Crown Street, which ran north to south down to the parade and the harbour.

Louis pointed on the map to the road that climbed up Fairlight Down and turned east towards Winchelsea and the border with Kent.

"This is the way they'll come," he said. "Morley won't be expecting to meet any resistance, so he'll take the quickest road."

"Then we surprise him here, before he reaches the village. An ambush." Liney Roach's bony finger stabbed at a spot on the map.

"No," said Louis. "Not out in the open. We must draw them in, fight them on our ground. Know your enemy, gentlemen, that's the secret of warfare. Think as they think, then do what they least expect. What do we know of this man Moses?"

"A savage," said Dr Rankin contemptuously. "And the men who follow him are a pack of wolves. Beggars, gypsies and robbers, all of them, the scum of the marshes. They think they're beyond the reach of the law."

"Morley will have expected us to strike a bargain," said Roach. "He won't be reckoning on a fight."

"Good," said Louis. "Let him think we're unprepared. Let him ride right into the heart of the village without meeting any resistance. At the bottom of the hill we'll set up a barricade here and defend it with twenty men."

He pointed on the map to the foot of Market Street where it turned into the parade.

"Twenty men? We'll be easy meat!" protested Roach. "If Morley's as good as his word, they'll be well armed and riding horses. How can twenty of us stand against them with the sea at our back and nowhere to run?"

"That is just how Morley will see it," said Louis.

"They'll come pouring down the hill like hounds chasing a fox."

"What then?" asked Dr Rankin.

"Then we open fire from both sides of the street. From these houses, where the rest of our men will be hidden at the windows, waiting for my command."

"A trap, by God!" said Roach, the light dawning in his wrinkled face.

"Precisely," said Louis. "The horses and men will be packed close together – perhaps four or five abreast. They'll be trapped by the houses, with nowhere to turn."

Liney Roach nodded his head. "Clever, if it works. But there's one thing you've forgotten, Napoleon."

"Which is?"

"Muskets. From that range we'll need muskets to do any damage. Pistols are no use and for that matter we've precious few of them."

Will had been listening so quietly and intently that they had almost forgotten he was there, but suddenly he thumped his hand flat on the table. "The Customs House!" he said.

They all looked at him in surprise.

"There are muskets kept in a storeroom at the back. They're issued to the volunteers but Lieutenant Lock ordered they should be kept under lock and key at night."

"Are you sure? How do you know this, Will?" asked the doctor.

"James Debney told me. He used to talk when he was staying here and the drink had loosened his tongue."

"A fine young man," smiled Louis. "His jacket keeps me warm at nights."

"Well, thank God for young Debney!" said Rankin.

"And for you, Will," added Louis, smiling at him. "You may just have given us a chance."

There was no time to lose. Louis said they must go right away to the Customs House to break into the storeroom. They would take as many muskets and rounds of ammunition as they could carry between them. If one of Lock's men was on guard duty, he would have to be dealt with. Roach and Dr Rankin agreed and got ready to leave. Will noticed they had already accepted Louis as their general and acted on his orders without question.

Will thought they made an unlikely triumvirate, the tall Frenchman in his borrowed clothes, flanked by the burly doctor and the hunched old undertaker with his white hair and spindly legs. Will wanted to go with them to the Customs House, but Louis shook his head, insisting that he should get some sleep.

"I'll have a task for you in the morning," he said. "One I can't trust to anyone else. Someone will have to keep a lookout on the road, to warn us when Morley's on his way."

"I can watch from the East Hill," suggested Will. "You can see as far as Fairlight Down, where the road comes over the hill."

"Good," said Louis. Will felt proud that such an important task had been entrusted to him. He noticed how Louis spoke to each person, making them feel their role was vital. Now he turned to Susannah, who so far had said nothing. "I need your help too, Mrs Finch. When they come I want the women and children somewhere safe, out of harm's way."

"There's St Michael's – the church on the hill," said Susannah. "I can pass the word tomorrow. But what if they won't leave their houses?"

"Tell them Morley means to burn down the village. Put the fear of God into them if you have to, just make sure they go. When Will returns I'll send him up to you."

Will thought at first he must have misheard.

"To the church? But I'll be with you!"

Louis shook his head. "Not this time, Will. You're too young. When this is over I don't want to be picking through the bodies in the street looking for you. Go to the church and help your mother. You'll be safe there." He saw the disappointment on Will's face. "Those are my orders, Will, I expect you to obey."

Will looked away and said nothing. He watched the three men take their leave of his mother and slip out into the dark street, where they would climb the hill towards the Customs House. Once he was safe in his room upstairs, he searched inside the straw of the mattress and pulled out the pistol he kept hidden there. It felt solid and reassuring in his hand and he practised aiming it at the door, with his arm fully extended. Before he lay down to sleep, he made sure it was primed and slipped it into the pocket of his coat.

17

Battle of Lydwell

Will screwed up his eyes, trying to keep them focused on the horizon. A mile to the north, Fairlight Down rose steeply, and a road curved over the brow of the hill, from this distance no more than a thin brown line. He had been watching the turnpike for the past four hours and was already numb with cold. Noon had passed long ago – the time that Morley had fixed for them to send their reply – but there had been no sign of any horsemen. He jumped down from the stone wall and stamped his feet, trying to bring some life back into them. Watching from the vantage point of the East Hill, he could see the world spread out below him like a green patchwork sea, vast and unending. Sheep grazed on the far side of the field by a copse of hawthorn trees, taking no interest in him. It seemed impossible to believe that in the streets below men were setting up a barricade and taking up their posts at windows. Will wondered if Lieutenant Lock had discovered yet that the Customs House had been broken into the previous night and fifty muskets belonging to the Lydwell Sharpshooters had dis-appeared. No one had told Lock about the business with Morley – he had asked questions in the village about the murder of Billy Hayes but as usual had been met by a wall of silence and distrust. This was an affair between smugglers – nothing to do with the law or the Revenue.

Will climbed back on to the stone wall and resumed his vigil. He was beginning to wish that Louis had chosen someone else to be the lookout. Perhaps Morley would not come after all. Perhaps the note they'd found on Billy Hayes's body had merely been intended to scare them into capitulating. Behind him two black crows rose into the sky from the thicket of hawthorn trees, splitting the air with their harsh cries. Something had startled them and Will instinctively felt for the pistol in his pocket. He caught sight of someone moving behind the line of the trees and when they stepped into the open he had the pistol raised, though his arm wasn't as steady as it should have been.

Hannah stopped in her tracks and, seeing the look on his face, let out a short laugh. "You look scared out of your wits."

"It's not funny. I could have killed you," said Will. "You shouldn't go creeping up on me. What are you doing up here anyway?"

"I came to see you. I thought you'd be hungry."

She showed him the bundle she'd brought with her. Inside the cloth was half a loaf of bread and a slice of cold tongue. He should have noticed the hurt in her eyes when she sat down on the wall next to him, but he hadn't eaten anything since breakfast and paid her no attention. He tore off a hunk of the dark brown bread and ate it hungrily, speaking between mouthfuls.

"You're supposed to be at the church."

Hannah lifted her shoulders and let them sag. "I'm not going."

"My mother's there," said Will. "Louis said. . ."

"I don't care what he said! I'm not going so don't try to make me. If Morley comes, I'm going to be there. I want to see him die!"

Will was taken aback by the violence of her outburst, and noticed for the first time the redness around her eyes. She had been crying.

"What is it? What's happened?" he asked.

She shook her head quickly and wiped her eyes with the back of her hand. Then she fumbled in her pocket and brought out a folded letter which she thrust at him. As soon as Will saw the writing and recognized it as the childish hand of Mrs Burrell he guessed what was in it. He read the first few lines:

My dearest Hannah, I have been dreading this day for so long. Last night your poor father...

Ned Burrell had lost his long battle with the fever, two nights after they had left Crowhurst. Will looked at Hannah's numb face. She was wearing her pale blue cotton dress and seemed oblivious to the biting wind that whipped her hair across her face. Her fingers twisted in and out of each other in her lap. Will guessed that she would be bitterly regretting having returned to Lydwell. If she hadn't listened to her mother, she could have stayed in Crowhurst and would have been at her father's bedside when he died. She kept her eyes fixed on some point on the far horizon, as if she had forgotten Will was there. He had lost a father himself, but he was only four years old when it happened, too young to feel the pain of his loss. He didn't know the right words to comfort her and held out the letter to her awkwardly. But she jumped down from the wall, pointing to the road coming over the brow of Fairlight Down. "Look! Look there!"

He followed her gaze and caught sight of what at first looked like a dark cloud smudging the horizon. As he watched, the cloud grew and thinned out, resolving itself into distinct shapes – men on horseback coming over the hill, at first a small group, then followed by more and more till the cloud became black and continuous like a swarm of locusts on the move. The horses were moving at a fast trot, their hooves stirring the dust on the road, which formed the cloud around them. He tried to count them but there were too many and they were followed by men who came on foot. In his heart he knew that the men standing behind their barricades in the street below would not be enough. Louis had underestimated the numbers that Morley could call on, either through threats or bribery.

This was not a raiding party, it was a small army.

Hannah was tugging at his arm urgently, pulling him away.

"Will! Come on! We must warn them."

It took them only a few minutes to reach the path descending the East Hill. Will was in front, running so fast down the grassy slope that he felt his heart pounding against his ribs. Hannah came after him, picking up her skirts, trying to keep up with him.

Even as they reached the edge of the village and clattered down Tithe Alley between the houses, Will was trying to shout, summoning all the breath left in his lungs: "They're coming! They're coming!"

When they reached the foot of Market Street, he saw they were waiting for him and Dr Rankin stepped out to catch him by the shoulders as he tried to slow down. Will pointed back the way he had come but for a few seconds couldn't find the breath to speak.

"You're sure it's Morley?" said Rankin.

Will nodded.

"Where? How far away?"

"A mile," he panted. "Coming over the Down. They'll be here soon."

Hannah arrived red-faced and a little annoyed that she hadn't been the first to break the news.

"How many?" asked Louis. "Did you count them?"

Will shook his head. "Too many. Maybe eighty, a hundred – I don't know."

Louis glanced at Dr Rankin and it was plain from his face that he hadn't expected so many. He put a hand on Will's shoulder. "You've done well, now it's up to us."

He nodded in Hannah's direction. "Take your friend up to the church where she'll be safe."

"I'm staying here," said Hannah firmly.

"We both are," said Will.

Louis saw the fierce determination in their faces.

He glanced up the hill. There wasn't time to argue and, in any case, he was hardly in a position to turn them away. Counting the men hidden either side of the road, he had only fifty-two in all, perhaps half as many as the enemy. Some of the smugglers had found reasons to leave the village that morning because they were terrified of Morley, while others had listened to Tom Ballard and stayed on their farms.

"All right," said Louis. "Stay behind the barricade but for the love of God keep your heads down when the fighting starts. You will fire only on my order. Aim for the chest, not the head. That way you've more chance of hitting the target."

He handed Will one of the Brown Bess muskets looted from the Customs House the previous night and showed him how to hold it, left hand under the barrel and the right just below the lock.

Hannah waited to be given a musket too but was told that her job was to help reload the muskets and have them ready for those manning the barricades. Will could see she wanted to argue, but Louis spoke to her like a commanding officer and she found herself obeying the authority in his voice. Soon she was learning how to load the musket, biting open the twisted paper cartridges that contained the bitter black gunpowder and ball.

Will took his place at the barricade next to Dr Rankin, standing behind a farm cart which had been turned on its side and smelled of hay and animals. Looking along the barricade he could see it stretched right across the bottom of the street, composed mainly of stout oak barrels stacked two deep and piled high with sacks, wooden crates and pieces of lumber so that it reached above head height. Anything that could be found and put to use had been pressed into service. All along the length of this ramshackle wall, men were making their last preparations or staring intently towards the top of the hill. With himself and Hannah, he counted twenty-one in all – men who he had often walked beside in the still hours of the morning, bringing back contraband from one of the coves dotting the coast. Most of them looked scared and on edge, fidgeting with their muskets, looking along the sights. Will guessed that most of them had never held a musket in their hands before, let alone been asked to fire one at an enemy. They were fishermen and farm hands, not soldiers. He wondered if, when the time came, many of them would turn and flee towards the sea behind them. His own mouth was dry and he tried to remember what Louis had taught him about tucking the butt of the musket into his shoulder and bracing himself for the sharp recoil when he fired. Next to him, a rat-faced man he knew only as Deakin took out a medal from beneath his shirt and kissed it. Will caught his eye and he grinned sheepishly, revealing small pointed teeth. "Saint Christopher," he said. "Never let me down yet."

The sky was overcast, with a dark mass of cloud to the south heralding the approach of rain. Rankin scratched his wiry hair, salted with grey, having left his doctor's wig at home this morning. "Where are they?" he asked. "Why don't they come?"

Something caught the light in an upper-storey window halfway up the street, and Will saw someone sliding the barrel of a musket into position. He recalled that Louis had hidden a dozen men in the bakery under the command of Job Moss and the rest in the Swan Inn on the opposite side of the street. The men crouching at the windows would be glad they weren't down below. It would be those behind the barricade who would take the brunt of the attack and if Morley's riders breached their wall, they would be defenceless and cut to pieces. Will prayed that Louis's plan would work. Looking at the anxious faces beside him, it seemed like a enormous gamble.

Dr Rankin's voice broke into his thoughts. "There's something I'd like to know, Will. That night Morley came to the Angel, he brought a lantern. Had you seen it before? Were you ever at that house where the gold was hidden?"

The question took Will completely by surprise and he couldn't think how to answer.

"If you knew something, I trust you would tell me?" persisted Rankin. Will was aware the doctor was studying him closely and, sooner or later, he would have to turn his head and face him.

"Of course," he replied. "What has it to do with me?"

"That's what I've been asking myself," said Rankin. "But I remember you looked mighty guilty that night, and if I didn't know you better, I'd say you were looking guilty now."

"It wasn't his fault, Dr Rankin, it was mine." Hannah's voice took both of them by surprise. Will hadn't realized she was standing behind them listening.

"Your fault, Hannah?" said Rankin.

"Yes. It was me who took the gold." Briefly she described what had happened the day they'd come upon the abandoned cottage in the wood. "If we had known it belonged to Morley, we'd have left it in that hole under the floor. But don't blame Will. I wanted the money for my father's sake. I thought it might save him."

Dr Rankin breathed out deeply. The face he turned towards them was even ruddier than usual, a sure sign that he was angry. "If you'd told me this before, you might have saved us all a deal of trouble," he said. "Even Billy Hayes's life. Who knows? We might even have bargained with Morley and prevented all this. Where is the damned money now?"

Hannah looked at Will. Neither of them wanted to confess the awful truth that they didn't know. It was a relief when they were interrupted by a loud disturbance to their right. Lieutenant Lock had appeared from somewhere and was trying to wrestle the musket from Deakin, who was fighting manfully to hold on to it.

"What in God's name are you doing?" thundered Rankin, venting all his anger on the Riding Officer.

"This, sir, is the property of the King, as you know damn well," blustered Lock. "Last night the Customs House was broken into and fifty muskets were stolen. I order you to hand them over now or face the consequences."

"Shut that prattling fool up or I'll put a bullet through his head!" Louis had come over and he had his pistol raised to show he was serious. Lieutenant Lock stared at the Frenchman, unable to believe the evidence of his own eyes.

"What the devil. . .? Will someone explain what is going on?" he spluttered. But before he could say more a shout went up from the barricade and they saw the enemy was in sight. Morley had drawn up his forces at the top of the hill by the schoolhouse, riders in front, musketeers on foot behind. They stretched across the road, row upon row, the horses so close together that their flanks were almost touching. The riders gripped their reins in one hand and urged their mounts forward at a slow trot.

Behind the barricade, Will waited for them to come. There were too many, he thought. Even if they were lucky and brought down some of the riders in the first wave of the attack, the next wave would be upon them in no time and sweep aside their barricade as if it was made of matchwood. To his left he saw Lieutenant Lock poke a musket through a gap in the barricade, having finally grasped that the village was genuinely under attack.

Will could hear Louis trying to instil courage into his inexperienced troops. "When they come down that hill you'll want to open fire, but hold back, wait for my order. It doesn't matter if you feel afraid. Do not run. Stand firm and fire on my command. Think of your women and children up at the church. You're fighting for them."

The enemy were coming steadily down the hill, without increasing their pace. About three hundred yards away they came to a halt, level with the Customs House. One of the riders detached himself from the main body and trotted forward on his tall chestnut horse to survey the barricade at the foot of the hill. Even from this distance Will could recognize the unmistakable figure of Moses Morley. From his high vantage point Morley would be able to see the heads behind the barricade, and would know that his forces were far superior. But he would also see that he'd have to send his men down the narrow street, with the shops and houses hemming them in on both sides. The attack would have to be swift and brutal.

Louis had his telescope trained upon the enemy.

"What are they waiting for?" he murmured impatiently. "Why don't they come?"

"Perhaps Morley is not such a fool," said Dr Rankin. "He suspects something."

But even as he spoke, Will saw Morley's arm raised in the air and heard the answering shout from the ranks of his riders as they urged their mounts forward and came pouring down the hill. They pressed their boots into the flanks of their horses and bent low over their necks, whipping them into a gallop. Four or five of the riders hit the front and Will could see their coat-tails flying out behind them and the dirt kicked up from the muddy street.

"Make ready!" ordered Louis.

Will brought his musket to full cock and rested his finger on the trigger, praying that Louis would give the order to fire soon.

"Hold, hold. Let them come," Louis was saying.

Will could feel the ground shaking under his feet and the barrels and boxes in the barricade rattling like the bones of the dead. Three hundred paces, two hundred and the riders were nearing the bakery and the Swan Inn, where the men hidden at the windows would be taking aim.

Now. Surely now, Will thought, fearing they had waited too long or lost their nerve.

When the volley of shots came from both sides of the street it was like a roll of thunder. Some horses went down in the front and the riders pitched over their heads, disappearing from sight. Those following behind tried to swerve aside at the last moment, but there was no room in the narrow street and their horses reared in the air or stumbled and fell over the bodies in front of them.

"Open fire!" bellowed Louis and the next volley of shots came from behind the barricade, Will firing with the rest into the chaos ahead of him and feeling the jolting kick of the musket against his shoulder. By chance one of the riders had got through and Will saw him hurtling towards them and a plume of smoke as he fired the pistol in his hand at point-blank range. To his right, he heard Deakin's cry and saw him fall back from the barricade. For a moment Will thought the rider was going to try and leap the barricade but, finding himself all alone, he pulled on his reins and tried to turn his horse about to go back. Lieutenant Lock took careful aim with his musket and let fly, and a second later the rider hung from his saddle lifeless, slumping to the ground as the frightened horse cantered away.

Will saw the riders in the second and third wave of the attack had given up all ambition of reaching the barricade. They were pouring back up the hill, passing Morley's musketeers, who followed their lead and ran in retreat without having fired a shot. The whole skirmish must have lasted no more than a few minutes and Will found himself gazing in disbelief at the devastation they had caused in that short space of time. A hundred paces away the street was littered with bodies of men and horses, while a number of the wounded were being helped back up the hill by their companions.

Will had only discharged his musket once, but now it was over he found his whole body was shaking. He put down his weapon and sank back heavily against the farm cart.

Hannah was in front of him and clasped him tight, hugging him with relief.

"We did it, Will! We did it! Look, they're running like frightened sheep!" A loud cheer went up from the men behind the barricade and was echoed from both sides of the street by the smugglers standing at their windows. At the top of the hill, Will could see the figure on the chestnut horse watching his humiliated troops return.

18

Smoke and Fire

Dr Rankin's ruddy face glowed with perspiration. "By heaven, we taught those scoundrels a lesson! They never knew what hit them! And it's you we have to thank, Louis. Look at them run!"

The Crowhurst men were indeed falling back from the Customs House and disappearing over the brow of the hill. The men at the barricade sent them on their way with taunts and jeers, elated by their unexpected victory. Only Louis watched them go impassively, reloading his pistol.

"Get some rest while you can," he said. "The next time it won't be so easy."

Dr Rankin looked at him in surprise. "The next time? You think they'll be back?"

"I'd stake my life on it, Doctor," replied Louis. "We have won a skirmish, that's all, but the battle is still to come. Morley underestimated us the first time, but he won't make the same mistake again."

Dr Rankin nodded and turned his attention to poor Deakin, who had taken a bullet in the chest and looked in a bad way. Will saw the blackened edge to the wound where the ball had ripped through Deakin's shirt below his lucky medal. He turned away while the doctor crouched over his patient and did the little he could to help him. Louis was moving amongst the men, urging them to keep alert. Beckoning to Will, he asked him to take a message to Job Moss and Liney Roach, telling them to hold their positions and stay alert for a second attack. Will was glad to have something to do other than watching and waiting.

As he slipped out from behind the barricade, dusk was gathering and the houses further up the hill had begun to lose their shape and substance. He had to pass some of the bodies in the street to reach the Swan Inn and gave them a wide berth, keeping close to the buildings. He found Liney Roach in an upstairs bedroom of the Swan Inn, watching from a window. The old undertaker was in good spirits, saying they would give Morley "a good roasting" if he dared to show his ugly face again. None of his men had suffered any casualties. The trap Louis had set had worked better than any of them could have hoped.

Crossing the street Will delivered the same message to Job Moss on the third floor of the tall, three-story building which housed the bakery. Having completed his mission, he was anxious to get back to the safety of the barricade. If a second attack came, he did not want to be caught in the open.

He was about to descend the hill when a bright spark of light caught his attention, flickering beyond the schoolhouse. At first he thought it was a lantern in a window, but when he caught sight of it again it was moving along the horizon and it seemed to split in two. A second later it vanished again and Will wondered if his weary eyes and the fading light were beginning to play tricks on him. He stole down the alleyway beside the bakery, hoping to get a clearer view away from the tall buildings of Market Street. Here the Lydden stream tumbled down towards the sea in a shallow gully, flowing over bottles, tin kettles and broken shards of pot before disappearing under a footbridge. Will stood on the bridge, gazing up the hill in the direction he had first glimpsed the light. This time he saw it clearly and understood what it meant. The red spark was a flaming torch and there was not one but two, coming swiftly down the hill towards him. Men on horseback. They were following the shallow stream than ran behind the houses, so their approach would be hidden from the enemy behind the barricade.

Will felt in his pocket for the pistol he had put there the night before. There was only a matter of seconds to make up his mind. He could run back to the barricade and alert Louis to the danger, but then he would be too late to stop the horsemen, for some instinct told him what Morley had in mind. He was going to set the bakery ablaze, knowing full well the men on the third storey would be trapped inside the building.

Will gripped the pistol, feeling its weight in his hand, trying to remember what Louis had taught him about keeping a steady arm, aiming low. A pistol didn't possess the range or accuracy of the sturdy Brown Bess and he had never fired this one before. He would have to wait till they were close. But if he could bring down the first rider, perhaps the second would panic and turn back. As they rounded the bend he would have a few seconds to take them by surprise – that was his only chance. He knew he might die in the attempt, but there was no time to consider that. The lives of a dozen men in the bakery depended on him.

With a drumming of hooves the first horseman came into view. He splashed through the shallow stream at a canter, the torch held in one hand like a red banner streaming in the wind. Will was close enough to see the astonished look on the rider's face as he saw the boy standing on the bridge with the pistol pointing at him. Will squeezed the trigger and heard the pistol crack, the recoil jarring his hand. But in his haste, he had fired too soon and too high – the shot missed its target, whistling harmlessly past. The horse must have been startled by the gun's report because it reared up on its hind legs and its rider lurched backwards from the saddle. He landed heavily in the stream, his head striking the stones with a sickening crunch and did not rise again.

There was no time for relief. Will struggled to reload his pistol, spilling the powder in his haste. Far too soon the second rider came into view, swerving sharply aside to avoid the riderless horse in the stream. Seeing the boy on the wooden bridge he urged his horse forward, coming straight for him. Will saw the torch raised high above his head and the scorching blow aimed at his face. He put up an arm to protect himself and, stepping backwards, lost his footing on the bridge, falling down into the icy, rushing water below.

The fall probably saved his life – he came up gasping with a mouthful of filthy water, and his knees and elbow painfully bruised. There was no sign of his attacker, but the sound of breaking glass told him all he needed to know. Clambering back on to the bridge, he was in time to see the horseman wheeling away and a bright light spilling from the ground floor window of the bakery. The building was on fire.

One glimpse through the window told him the fire was already spreading fast in the back room, where he could see the great ovens and sacks of flour stacked against a wall. Once the flames took hold, the old timber-framed building would collapse like a deck of cards. He tried the back door but found it locked. When he hammered on it with his fists, there was no answer from within. Back through the alleyway he ran, fearing that he was already too late. When he burst in through the front door the smoke was so thick that it forced him to cover his mouth with his handkerchief. He gasped a warning, choking out the words. "Fire! Fire!"

Through the open doorway of the shop he could see the leaping flames in the back room and hear the crackle and spit of burning timber. He fought his way through the smoke to reach a passageway, where the wooden staircase led to the upper storeys. Even as he reached the foot of the stairs a beam of wood dropped from the ceiling so that he had to leap back to avoid it. Flames had begun to lick hungrily round the banisters.

"Get out! Get out, before it's too late!" he cried up the stairs.

Job Moss appeared at the top, plainly bewildered by the catastrophe that had overtaken the building so quickly.

Will could only guess that the men on the third floor had been so intent on watching the hill for the enemy that they hadn't noticed the smoke until it began to seep upstairs and issue into the street. He heard voices raised in alarm as they finally realized the danger.

"What happened?" asked Moss.

"Never mind. Get them out, Job, while there's still time!" Will urged him.

Will tried to stamp out the flames around him but there were too many. A few minutes more and the whole lower part of the staircase would be a wall of flame, leaving no escape for those trapped on the upper floors. The blacksmith reappeared with a dozen men behind him, pushing and jostling in their panic. They came stumbling down the stairs in their heavy boots, clutching their muskets and leaping over the flames at the bottom to reach the safety of the corridor. Some climbed over the banisters and dropped the last six feet into the passageway below.

"This way! Hurry!" Will shouted back to them. Coughing and choking, they fought their way out of the blaze, through the smoke-filled shopfront, where glass jars and pots on the shelves were exploding like grapeshot. When they staggered out into the street,

Will could see smoke billowing from the windows and the tall building lit up from the inside like a giant lantern. Job bent over with his hands clasping his knees, retching from the acrid fumes. He spat into the dust for good measure.

"Morley did this," he said.

Will nodded. "I'm sorry Job, they came down the stream. I tried to stop them."

"Sorry?" The blacksmith shook his head ruefully. "Strike me, lad, if you hadn't warned us, we'd all be burned to a crisp by now. There's not many would risk their necks like you did."

They watched as part of the ceiling gave way with a crash that seemed to shake the whole building. Above the crackling of the fire, Will caught the sound of voices raised in warning. At the foot of the hill men were standing on top of the barricade and waving frantically. At first Will thought they were pointing to the danger of the fire spreading – the bakery stood on its own, but a spark carried by the wind could land on a roof, starting a blaze that would threaten the whole village. But the danger came from another direction. Will caught sight of Hannah's blue dress as she clambered over the barricade and ran a few yards towards them. Some instinct made him turn then and he saw them coming from the top of the hill. Morley's riders. The fire had done its work, flushing them out into the open, spreading confusion among them; now Morley intended to finish them off.

"The barricade! Fall back!" Job was bellowing as if he was a sergeant-at-arms. Most of the men had already seen the danger and had broken into a run. Will was near the front, quicker into his stride than some of the older men, fear overcoming the weariness in his legs. If the riders caught up with them they would be cut down, shot in the back or, worse, trampled under the thundering hooves of the horses. All around him men were running pell-mell for the barricade, feeling the ground begin to shake as their pursuers gained on them.

At the bottom of the hill Will caught sight of Hannah in her pale blue dress, urging them to hurry. He was relieved when hands reached out from the barricade and caught her under the arms, lifting her to safety. Only fifty paces now, but glancing back over his shoulder he could see their pursuers plunging through the black smoke that billowed across the road from the bakery. A ragged volley of shots rang out from behind them, and Will remembered that Liney Roach and his men were still at the upper windows of the Swan Inn, firing down on the ranks of the enemy. He saw the first man to reach the barricade clamber on top of the barrels and leap over, disappearing from sight. Others were doing the same, throwing their bodies over in their haste to get under cover. Hands reached out to him and the next moment he had his foot on the side of the farm cart and had landed hard on the other side. He caught sight of Hannah's relieved face as he scrambled to his feet. There was no time to exchange words, she turned back to her task of ramming a ball home into the muzzle of a gun. Will found a musket thrust into his hands by Dr Rankin and took his place among the men lining the barricade.

The first wave of the attack was already thundering towards them, seven or eight riders with the rest strung out in pursuit, and behind them Morley's foot soldiers, running down the hill in a ragged line. Will tried to swallow but his throat was parched and he could still taste the bitter smoke in his mouth. The hooves drummed in his ears and the barricade once again began its frightening death rattle. *Surely this time they'll sweep us away, cut through us like waves of corn,* Will thought to himself. He squinted along the barrel of the Brown Bess and swallowed an impulse to cast it aside and run, run anywhere away from the charge that was about to engulf them.

"Stand firm, stand firm," muttered Louis behind him. "Anyone who leaves his post, I'll shoot them myself. Make ready . . . *Open fire!*" the last words were screamed and the first volley of shots erupted from the barricade. Some of the horses and their riders went down immediately but others came on. Briefly Will caught sight of Morley on his chestnut horse, urging his men forward with a pistol in his hand. Then, as the first horses reached the barricade, all was chaos and confusion. Some tried to leap the wall confronting them, but Louis had built it high, so that the frightened beasts floundered into it. Only one rider made it over and Will saw him dragged from his horse by Louis and despatched before he could get away. The horses that had baulked at the jump wheeled around, whinnying and snorting with fear, their riders struggling to regain control. They were trapped between the barricade and the advance of the oncoming riders, easy targets for those firing from behind the wall. Will saw the face of a red-haired man suddenly loom over the top of the barricade and a pistol pointing down towards him. He struck out with the butt of his musket and the face disappeared backwards with a cry. All along the line of the barricade the marsh smugglers were trying to clamber over but were driven back by those defending the wall. Will doubted if they could hold out for long and once the line was breached Morley's men would pour through like a river.

When he saw a fresh wave of men swarm down the hill, emerging from the smoke like grey ghosts, he thought the battle was lost. It took a few seconds for it to dawn on him that it was Liney Roach, whose men had left the Swan Inn to attack from the rear as Louis had instructed them. Now Morley's army found itself encircled, caught between the enemy at the barricade and those who fired into their ranks from behind them. Seeing their heavy losses, many of the horsemen took their only means of escape, weaving their way through the chaos and back up the hill. The tide had turned and when Louis ordered his men forward, the sight of the Lydwell men pouring through a gap in the barricade was too much for their demoralized foe. Those that remained on the street abandoned the fight and fled. Will pursued them with the rest, running as if he would never stop.

Halfway up the hill he slowed his pace, suddenly aware that most of the men had given up the chase long ago and he'd left them behind. He had his pistol in his hand, having reloaded before he left the barricade. Now he found himself alone in the dark clouds of smoke that billowed across the road from the bakery, almost blinding him. After the din of the battle, the silence seemed unnatural, broken only by distant shouts, and the thumps and cracks coming from the burning building. He called out to see if anyone was in earshot but in answer heard the snort of a horse close at hand. It came out of the smoke and flames, trotting slowly towards him, the rider holding the reins in one hand, a tall, powerfully-built man on a chestnut horse. Will knew it was Morley before he saw the cold eyes and the scarred, ugly face. The horse shook its head and came to a halt, its flanks glossy with sweat. Morley pulled a pistol from his belt. He was in no hurry, the boy was unarmed and all alone. He recognized him as the brat he'd seen at the Angel – Rankin's little puppy. It would be a pleasure to put a bullet through his head.

Will knew that it was too late to try and run, Morley would shoot him in the back before he got ten yards. He'd left his musket behind: all he had was the pistol in his hand, which he kept behind his back. Morley was no more than ten paces away and taking his time, savouring the moment. Will cocked the pistol as he brought his arm up in one swift movement. He pulled the trigger but there was no answering flash or sound except the dull click of the hammer. With a sinking heart he realized that water must have got into the pistol's chamber when he fell off the bridge.

"Well, well," said Morley. "Looks like you ran out of luck."

It had begun to rain on them. Will knew he was going to die and closed his eyes, wanting to shut out the cruel pleasure he could read in Morley's face. When the pistol fired he heard the bullet whine through the air, but felt nothing. He opened his eyes to see Morley leaning over at a strange angle in his saddle, clutching at his right shoulder. He turned to see Hannah standing behind him. The musket was still smoking in her hand, and there was a look of blank surprise on her face. He ran to her in time to catch her as her legs folded and gave way. He thought she had fainted until he saw the dark stain on her blue dress and felt the warmth of the blood on his fingers. Morley must have seen her appear out of the smoke at the last moment and had fired just as she raised the musket.

Will knelt down in the rain beside her, an arm supporting her back. For a moment nothing came out of his mouth except broken sounds, then he heard a voice crying for help which sounded strangely unlike his own. Seconds or minutes passed before Lieutenant Lock came running, followed by Dr Rankin and some of the others. The doctor lifted Hannah gently from him and carried her, as limp as a rag doll, across the road towards the Swan Inn.

She was taken upstairs to a room with green velvet curtains and a fire laid in the grate that no one had lit. When Dr Rankin began to cut away Hannah's bloodied dress to look at the wound, Will felt he shouldn't be there and slipped away, closing the door softly behind him. Through the tall window over the staircase he could see that rain had begun to fall steadily in the street outside, dousing the flames that still burned across the street in the charred black remains of the bakery. It would prevent the fire from spreading any further. The village was safe, but Will hardly cared. If Hannah died, it would all have been for nothing.

19

Passage to France

Will climbed the zigzag path between the gorse bushes, coming up over the brow of the East Hill. It was early evening and in the valley below him the village was cloaked in darkness. A necklace of lights marked the curve of the bay where the lamps had been lit in many of the fishermen's cottages. Will often felt this was his favourite time of the day, when the village drew into itself, easing into the long hours of another winter evening. The parlour of the Angel Inn would be busy now, humming with talk. Flushed with ale, men would be recounting their own part in the battle of the streets two days before. Since that time, Morley hadn't been seen or heard of. Some said the gangleader had died of a gunshot he had received at the height of the struggle, and there were a few who boasted that they had fired the fatal shot themselves. Others claimed that Morley was still alive, but his days were numbered. A troop of redcoats had been sent into Kent, they said, to arrest the surviving members of the Crowhurst gang and bring their leader to trial.

Whatever the rumours, Will knew that Morley's cruel reign was over. News of the villagers' resistance had spread by word of mouth through all the surrounding countryside. A dramatic account of a battle waged openly in the streets between armed gangs of smugglers had even appeared in the *Brighton Gazette*. No one feared Morley any more. The story was recounted time and again, and always the recurring theme was the part played by the unknown Frenchman whom people said had been the architect and hero of the victory.

Now Will was making for the lime kilns, where he hoped to see Louis one last time. He had last seen his friend behind the barricade, urging them forward to put the enemy to flight, but at some point in the confusion that followed, Louis must have slipped away into the gathering darkness. Whatever part he had played in defending the village, he guessed that it wouldn't deter Lieutenant Lock from arresting him as soon as the battle was over. Lock had been beside himself with rage when he discovered his adversary had slipped through his fingers a second time. He had charged six of the villagers, including the undertaker, Roach, with breaking into the Customs House, but no witnesses came forward and no evidence could be produced to convict them. In addition, the men swore on their lives they had no knowledge of where the Frenchman would be hiding.

As he followed the coast path, Will reflected that in fact he still knew very little about Louis. His friend had recounted certain episodes of his life – his house in Paris, his childhood visits to his grandfather's house in Brighton – but these told him little. Louis had never spoken to Will about his years as an officer nor explained why he left the army. Now he was leaving and Will knew that it was unlikely he would ever see him again. Dr Rankin had told him about the boat that would slip into Stairhole Cove under the cover of darkness that night to take Louis across the Channel to France. It had all been arranged with the help of the smugglers as a gesture of their gratitude.

Passing the ruins of the lime kilns, Will left the path, picking his way over rough ground to climb out of the valley. The lantern he was carrying would be clearly visible from the sea but he hoped there weren't any naval gunboats patrolling the coast that evening. Stairhole Cove had been chosen because it was a remote inlet, which could only be reached with some difficulty on foot. Its isolation made it a favoured haunt of smugglers.

Reaching the cave, Will squeezed inside, inching his way through the narrow entrance. He whistled into the darkness as a signal to let Louis know that he was coming. When there was no reply he called out Louis's name. His voice echoed through the long, narrow chamber but no answer came back in reply. Will had never liked coming to this lonely place at night. It took an effort of will to enter the cave, where the cold walls pressed in on him and the stifling darkness threatened to swallow him up. He wondered how Louis could have slept there soundly at night on the hard stone floor with only the moaning of the wind for company.

Turning the bend in the passage, he reached the widest part of the cave and shone his lamp into the corners. The fire had been stamped out, but the embers still gave off a little warmth when he placed his hand over them, suggesting that Louis had been there recently. Will guessed he would be coming back, as his few belongings were collected together in a pile, ready for the journey home. There were the green jacket and breeches Louis had stolen from James Debney rolled up in a bundle, and beside them a bottle of brandy, almost empty, that Will had brought himself from the Angel's cellar. Underneath the clothes he found a seaman's chest, edged with brass at the corners. Will remembered seeing it once before, the day he had walked in on Louis and the bluejacket called Joseph. He set down the lamp on a ledge and squatted down to examine the chest. When he tried to lift it, it was surprisingly heavy for its size and something rattled inside like stones in a tin. He ran his fingers over the lid experimentally and tried the brass catch. It wasn't locked. Will knew he had no business searching through Louis's personal possessions but by now his curiosity was overwhelming. There was so much he didn't know about Louis, and perhaps this chest would provide some answers. If he heard footsteps in the passage he could quickly close the lid and cover the chest with the clothes.

The contents at first looked disappointing. There was Louis's telescope, a clasp knife and a tinder box, similar to the one Will carried himself. But wrapped in an oilskin cloth he found a map and a well-thumbed pocket book. This was more interesting. He remembered catching a glimpse of the book once before and recalled how Louis had been quick to hide it away. The pages were filled with rows of neat handwriting in black ink, but when he tried to read the words they were all in French and he could make no sense of them. As he turned the pages his eye fell on a long list of names with numbers alongside them.

The Griffin   *12*
The Monarch   *64*
The Pearl   *64*

They were the names of ships, that was plain enough, but the numbers were more puzzling. Will guessed they might have referred to the number of the crew on each ship or more likely, it suddenly dawned on him, the number of guns they carried. But what use was a list of naval vessels and their firepower to someone like Louis? Unless . . . he pushed the thought away, still unwilling to believe it. Turning his attention to the map, he unfolded it and held it up to the dim light of the lamp. It showed the south-east coast of England, stretching from Brighton in the west all the way to Dover. A map would have been valuable to Louis if he'd wanted to reach Brighton, but that didn't explain the series of small crosses marking beaches along the coast of Sussex and Kent.

Beyond these objects the chest contained nothing else of interest, though when he had first picked it up, he had been struck by its weight. On an impulse he knocked on the wooden base inside and found it made a hollow sound. Taking Louis's clasp knife, he slid it down between the base and the side of the chest. It levered up easily, revealing a hidden space below, four inches deep, that would have been missed in any cursory examination. Will stared at the bag lying in the bottom. It was made of sailcloth, now brown and discoloured, with a few small splinters of wood caught in the material. The shock of finding it there almost took his breath away. When he thrust his hand inside the leather purse, he brought out one of the leather purses inside. He emptied the contents into the bottom of the chest and stared at the glistening heap of gold guineas. Even in that cold, blind cave, they seemed to glow and give off a light of their own. The thought flashed into Will's mind that there was nothing to stop him taking the money. If he took the bag and returned home now, no one would ever know. Morley wouldn't be back for his gold and Louis had no more right to it than he did. But his eye fell on the evidence of the pocket book and the map. There were things here more important than gold, information that might cost thousands of lives. The truth could no longer be avoided – Louis was a thief and a liar. Worst of all, he was a spy. Even if Will couldn't read the contents of the pocket book, the list of ships and numbers could only mean one thing: Louis had been spying on the English fleet. He had been sent ahead to prepare the way for Napoleon's invasion, perhaps even to identify the beach where the French would land. In his ignorance Will had been helping a foreign spy, had fed and clothed him, even helped him to escape. How blind he had been! Looking back, he could see the warning signs he had wilfully ignored. The letters that

Louis had been so anxious to rescue from the wreck of the *Fortune* – what was really in them? Perhaps evidence that would have betrayed Louis's real identity. The bluejacket, Joseph, must have been one of Louis's spies, a traitor paid to bring him names and details of ships in port along the south coast.

In his agitation Will found he was pacing back and forth by the cold fire. He had blundered into something far more important than a local war between gangs of smugglers. Nothing less than the defence of England was at stake. Louis mustn't be allowed to escape, that was clear, and perhaps Will was the only person that could stop him.

He began to replace the contents of the chest, hurriedly cramming the shining guineas back into the purse. When he came to the map and the pocket book, however, he hesitated. He knew now what he had to do. The money didn't matter any more – it was smugglers' gold and had brought him nothing but trouble – but what was written in the book, that was beyond price. For all he knew, the success of the invasion depended on what Louis had found out. Making up his mind, he slipped the book inside his jacket pocket, with the map folded inside it. Yet, even as he knelt to replace the rest of the chest's contents, he heard a sound that made him raise his head. He kept quite still, listening. From somewhere along the passage he caught the scrape of metal against stone –

someone was entering the cave. As he got to his feet his hand flew to his left-hand pocket, where he kept the pistol he always carried with him, loaded in case of trouble.

If it came to it, he thought, he would have to kill Louis. The knowledge was like a hard stone in his belly.

The yellow eyes of the lamp emerged from the dark and a shadow fell across the wall. Louis stepped into view. His hand automatically went to the pistol at his belt, but when the light caught the boy's pale face, he let it drop to his side.

"Thank God! You startled me, Will. What are you doing here?"

He took in the pistol levelled at his chest and the nervous determination on the boy's face. The lid of the chest lay open with the pile of clothes spilled on the floor. It told him all he needed to know.

"So. You found out. What gave me away?"

"I found your book," Will replied, touching his pocket. There was no point in pretending.

"Ah, the book. It's nothing important. Just a diary I wrote to pass the long hours while I was here. All the same, if you've no objection, I'd like it back."

He was trying to act as if it didn't matter, but Will wasn't fooled.

"You're lying," he said. "I've seen what's in here. You've been lying to me from the day I met you."

Louis placed the lantern on the floor of the cave between them. "Come, Will, that's not fair. It's true that my grandfather lived in Brighton and I stayed there as a child. That's where I learned my English. I could even show you the house on Queen Street, though I admit you might be disappointed. It's not quite as grand as I described."

"But you didn't come here because of your grandfather's will, did you? You came because you're a spy."

Louis gave a weary shrug of his shoulders. "Even your English government has its own spies. A war isn't only fought on the battlefield alone. Letters, secrets, information – those are weapons of war." He spread his hands as if there was too much to explain. "Do you love your country, Will?"

"Of course."

"Then we are no different. Whatever I've done was in the service of France."

"And stealing gold?" asked Will. "Was that for France too?"

"There you're mistaken. It was you who stole it from me."

Will shook his head. "The gold belonged to Morley. I heard him say so myself."

"Morley was a fool. He was only the carrier, the pack horse. The money came from one of your London banking houses – 30,000 gold guineas in all."

He pointed at the chest. "What's in there is only a small part of it. Morley's part of the bargain was to see the money safely delivered."

"Where? To France?"

"To France, of course. My country needs gold to pay our armies, and we're prepared to pay a high price. That means there's a profit to be made in smuggling guineas. Even a jackal like Morley would have been well rewarded."

Will remembered Dr Rankin had called it the Guinea Run. Forty-foot boats crossing the channel, rowed by crews of smugglers and carrying enough gold for a king's ransom. So the money had been intended to pay French soldiers.

"That day we found the gold," said Will. "You were there at the house, weren't you?"

Louis nodded. "I was to meet a man called Tyler, one of Morley's men. He was bringing two hundred guineas and would arrange for the delivery of the rest. But nothing went to plan. You see the *Fortune* wasn't a merchant ship, Will."

That much Will had guessed. "It was carrying contraband," he said. He thought of the cask of brandy the two children had dragged ashore at Leonard's Cove.

"The cargo was promised to Morley," said Louis. "It was his payment, but when the ship went down it went to the bottom of the sea. When I tried to explain, this fellow Tyler flew into a rage. Accused me of trying to cheat them."

"You killed him," guessed Will.

"I had no choice, Will, believe me. He drew his pistol. When I saw he was dead, I decided to take the gold, leave while I had the chance. But then you turned up at the door."

"It was you we heard running away."

"What else could I do? I had just shot a man," said Louis. "I hid outside in the woods and kept watch on the house. I saw Morley leave empty-handed and then you and the girl sneaking off through the woods. I guessed that you must have found the gold."

"But I still don't understand," said Will. "How did you know where it was hidden?"

"It wasn't difficult to find out. I followed you back to the village and the priest's house."

The rest was easy to imagine. Louis had watched the Rectory and had seen Hannah hide the money in the tree. A few days later, when the house was empty, he had gone back to reclaim it.

"And now, my young friend, I must leave you," said Louis. "The boat will be waiting. But first I need that book you have in your pocket."

"No," said Will.

"Don't play games with me. I haven't much time."

He took one step closer, holding out his hand. Will raised the pistol and with his thumb cocked the hammer. The harsh click made Louis stop in his tracks and for the first time he looked uncertain.

"One step closer and I'll shoot you, I swear."

The pistol wavered slightly in his hand, but the muzzle was pointed straight at Louis's heart and from this range it would be impossible to miss.

"Come, Will. Whatever has happened, we're still friends."

Will shook his head. "You lied to me. You're my enemy."

"No, I don't think so," said Louis softly. He came one more step and Will's finger tightened on the trigger.

"Walk away," said Will. "I'm giving you the chance. Take your gold and whatever's in the chest, I won't stop you. But if you want this book, you'll have to kill me first."

For a few seconds Louis stood regarding him, weighing the situation. The lantern on the floor cast their shadows in monstrous shapes on the wall of the cave – two giants facing each other in combat. Will could see the pistol tucked into Louis's belt, beneath his coat. The moment the Frenchman reached for it, he would have to pull the trigger – there would be no choice. His arm ached and the curved butt of the pistol stuck to his hand with sweat. The silence stretched out between them.

Finally Louis raised his hands as if in surrender.

"All right. You give me no choice." He bent down to bundle the clothes inside the chest, closing the lid. "Goodbye, Will," said Louis. "Say farewell to your mother for me."

He hoisted the chest on to his shoulder and, without another word, turned away. Will watched him go, until his shadow was swallowed by the darkness and the echo of his footsteps died away.

As Will left the cave, he caught sight of a bright sliver of light, descending the path towards the headland and Stairhole Cove. Will slipped the pistol back into his pocket and felt the book there, small and hard. He wondered if, back there in the cave, he would have carried out his threat to pull the trigger. He doubted it – but perhaps Louis had known that all along.

20

Hannah

"**I** wondered when you'd be back."

"Can I see her?"

"She's still weak. Don't go working her up and getting her excited."

"But she's not going to die?"

"No, she's not going to die." Dr Rankin smiled. "Not now. She'll never know what a fortunate young woman she is. If the bullet had entered a few inches higher, it would have been a different story. But with time and rest, I believe she'll recover. You can go up, Will, she's been asking for you."

The doctor was standing at the foot of the stairs in the Rectory, with his ancient leather bag in his hand. He had been visiting his patient when Will happened to call at the door. On any other day Mrs Lawson, the pinch-faced housekeeper, would have sent the boy away with a flea in his ear, but the doctor had brushed aside her objections and forced her to let him in. As Will ascended the heavy oak staircase, he was conscious of her standing below in the hall watching him disapprovingly, noting the mud on his boots. He was glad when he reached the landing and heard the housekeeper's crisp steps retreating towards the kitchen.

A fire burned in the grate in the small bedroom, even though it was only mid-afternoon. Hannah was sitting up in bed in her white nightdress, her dark hair falling on the pillows propped behind her. In a week she seemed to have grown much thinner and smaller. Will tried to hide his dismay at the change in her appearance. When she looked up at him, though, it was the old Hannah, who couldn't decide whether to look pleased or cross.

"Why didn't you come before?" she demanded. "I've been cooped up in this room with no one to talk to."

"I called every day after school. Your uncle wouldn't let me in."

Hannah pulled a face. Her uncle hadn't said anything about his visits. "He comes in every morning and sits there by my bed. Stares and says nothing. I have to pretend I'm asleep so that he'll go away."

"Dr Rankin told me he's been sick with worry."

"Has he?" She looked pleased. "Well, I'm better now. The doctor showed me the bullet that he pulled out. I wanted to keep it, but my uncle took it away in the night."

Will was relieved that she could talk about what had happened without any hint of reproach. For the past week the possibility that she would die had hung over him like dark cloud, filling him with guilt and dread. He knew that Morley would have killed him that day on the hill, and only Hannah's courage had saved his life.

"Tell me everything that's happened," she said. "I've been lying here for days and they all treat me like a child. No one will tell me anything."

Will began to tell her what he knew. Morley was still alive, but reliable reports said he was in Maidstone gaol awaiting trial. No one expected him to escape the gallows. He went on to describe his encounter with Louis in the cave and what he'd discovered about his true identity. He told her of the chest with the gold guineas inside and the clues written in the pocket book, though he didn't reveal what became of it. Hannah listened with wide eyes, occasionally interrupting with a question. When he'd finished the whole story she looked thoughtful.

"I don't care if he is a spy," she said at last. "I'm glad you let him go."

Will nodded. "He'll be home now. In Paris – if that's where he really lives."

"That book you saw in the chest. You think it was important?"

Will smiled. He'd been keeping this part till last. "I don't know. Most of it's written in French," he said. He reached into his jacket pocket and drew out the grey book. When he placed it in her hands, a look of wonder spread over her face.

"You kept it!"

"Yes. He took the gold but I think this was what he really wanted."

Hannah leafed through the pages filled with Louis's neat handwriting and the lists containing names of English frigates and gunboats. She unfolded the map she found tucked inside the book and frowned at the crosses marked along the coast.

"Beaches." Will explained. "Perhaps they were looking for a place where the fleet could land."

"What are you going to do with this?" she asked.

"I don't know. Perhaps I should hand it over to Lieutenant Lock."

"Yes. But then you'd have to explain how you came by it."

"That might be difficult," he agreed. "And besides, everyone in the village will know that Louis was a spy. I'm not sure I want that."

Hannah looked at him, her eyes alive with mischief.

"I suppose," she said slowly. "I suppose we don't have to show it to anyone." She glanced at the fire burning in the grate.

Will took the pocket book from her and crossed to the fireplace. He held it between his thumb and forefinger, suspended by one corner over the bright flames. This way it would remain their secret. No one would ever know for sure who Louis Moreau was or why he came. In years to come they would only remember that, during the wars with Napoleon, a mysterious Frenchman had appeared and helped to save the village. It would become one of those stories that passed into local legend. Will let the book fall from his hand into the glowing red embers. He watched the pages curl at the edges and turn black, before the flames caught them and the book burned in a bright plume of yellow and blue. Wherever he was now, Will felt that Louis would approve.